WORKS ON PAPER

TRANSLATIONS BY ELIOT WEINBERGER

Octavio Paz, *Eagle or Sun?* (1970; revised edition 1976)
Octavio Paz, *Blanco* (1974)
Octavio Paz, *A Draft of Shadows and Other Poems* (1979)
Homero Aridjis, *Exaltation of Light* (1981)
Octavio Paz, *Selected Poems* (1984)
Jorge Luis Borges, *Seven Nights* (1984)
Octavio Paz, *The Four Poplars* (1985)

Eliot Weinberger

WORKS ON PAPER

1980–1986

A NEW DIRECTIONS BOOK

"Another Memory of Charles Reznikoff" first appeared in *Charles Reznikoff: Man and Poet*, edited by Milton Hindus (National Poetry Foundation). "At the Death of Kenneth Rexroth," reprinted from the Rexroth issue of *Sagetrieb*, appeared in *New Directions 49* and *The Pushcart Prize, XI*. "Octavio Paz" was the introduction to *Selected Poems of Octavio Paz* (New Directions). "The Spider & the Caterpillar" was the introduction to *The Name Encanyoned River: Selected Poems of Clayton Eshleman* (Black Sparrow Press). "Han Yu's Address to the Crocodiles" first appeared in *The Language of the Birds*, edited by David Guss, Copyright © 1985 by David Guss (North Point Press), reprinted by permission of the publisher. Ten of these essays were first presented in *Sulfur*; five in *Vuelta* (Mexico City). The others were originally published in *The Nation, Paideuma, The L.A. Weekly, Montemora, L'Autre Journal* (Paris), and *Syntaxis* (Tenerife). Most of the essays have been rewritten since these first appearances.

Grateful thanks is given for permission to quote from the following works: William Bronk, "The Strong Room of the House," *Life Supports* (Copyright © 1981 by William Bronk), published by North Point Press and reprinted by permission, all rights reserved; E. E. Cummings, "a kike is the most dangerous" (Copyright 1950 by E. E. Cummings), reprinted from *Complete Poems 1913–1962* by permission of Harcourt Brace Jovanovich, Inc.; Emily Dickinson, poems 566 and 872, *The Poems of Emily Dickinson*, edited by Thomas H. Johnson, Cambridge, Mass.: The Belknap Press of Harvard University Press (Copyright 1951, © 1955, 1979, 1983 by The President and Fellows of Harvard College), reprinted by permission of the publishers and the Trustees of Amherst College; Rachel Blau DuPlessis, "Otherhow" (Copyright © 1985 by Rachel Blau DuPlessis), cited by permission of the author; Carolyn Forché, "The Memory of Elena," "Photograph of My Room," "The Colonel," and "Message," *The Country Between Us* (Copyright © 1977, 1979, 1980, 1981 by Carolyn Forché), reprinted by permission of Harper & Row, Publishers, Inc.; Allen Ginsberg, "Genocide" (Copyright © 1968 by Allen Ginsberg), reprinted by permission of the author; Langston Hughes, "The Weary Blues," "Suicide's Note," "Gone Boys," and "Maybe," *The Selected Poems of Langston Hughes* (Copyright © 1959 by Langston Hughes), reprinted by permission of Alfred A. Knopf, Inc.; Langston Hughes, "White Man," *Good Morning Revolution* (Copyright © 1973 by Faith Berry), "Be-Bop Boys," and "Good Morning," *The Selected Poems of Langston Hughes* (Copyright © 1959 by Langston Hughes), reprinted by permission of Harold Ober Associates Incorporated; Randall Jarrell, "A Camp in a Prussian Forest," *The Complete Poems* (Copyright 1946 by Randall Jarrell; copyright © renewed 1974 by Mrs. Randall Jarrell), reprinted by permission of Farrar, Straus & Giroux, Inc.; Mary Ellen Mark, *Falkland Road: Prostitutes of Bombay* (Copyright © 1981 by Mary Ellen Mark), by permission of Alfred A. Knopf, Inc.; Wendy Doniger O'Flaherty, "The Brahmanas," *Women, Androgynes, and Other Mythical Beasts* (Copyright © 1980 by The University of Chicago Press), by permission of the publisher; Toby

Contents

I
INVENTIONS OF ASIA

II
EXTENSIONS OF POETRY

"As long as there is still-life, there is still hope"

—Wm. Merritt Chase

for N.S. & A.D.

WORKS ON PAPER

I
INVENTIONS
OF ASIA

The Dream of India

[c. 1492]

For India was named by Noah, and its king is called the King of Knowledge.

For Paradise is in India, and in Paradise is the living fountain from which the four great rivers flow.

In India a year has two summers and two winters.

In India the land is always green.

Shadows there fall south in summer and north in winter.

In India there are twelve thousand seven hundred islands, some made entirely of gold, and some of silver. There is an island where pearls are so plentiful the people wear no clothes, but cover themselves in pearls.

In India wine is made from the milk of palmtrees. There is a tree whose fruit is a kind of bread.

In India there is a worm which cannot live without fire.

Snakes crawl about in the streets there.

In India they sleep on mattresses of silk on beds of gold. They eat at tables with silver vessels, and everyone, no matter of what rank, wears pearls and rings with precious stones.

There is a race of people there with eight toes on each foot and eight fingers on each hand. Their hair is white until they are thirty, and then it begins to turn black.

They have no poor people there, and all strangers are welcome.

In India crabs turn to stone the minute they are exposed to air.

There is a race of people there who live on the smell of an apple. And when they travel they must take an apple with them, for without the smell of it they will die.

It was so hot the people never left their houses.

Horses there are few and wretched, for they are fed with boiled meat and boiled rice.

In India they have a class of philosophers devoted to astronomy and the prediction of future events. And I saw one among them who was three hundred years old, a longevity so miraculous that wherever he went he was followed by children.

There are no liars there.

In India it is the custom for foreign traders to stay at inns. There the food is cooked for the guest by the landlady, who also makes the bed and sleeps with the stranger.

There is a race of people whose ears hang down to their knees.

In India there is a fountain guarded by deadly snakes. It is the only water in that place, and if anyone wishes to drink, he must take off all his clothes, for the snakes fear nudity more than fire.

There is a race of people there whose upper lip is so large they cover their faces with it when they sleep in the sun.

And I saw a king walking with two men before him sounding trumpets; two men behind him holding colored parasols over his head to shade him from the sun; and on each side of him a panegyrist, each rivaling the other in his invention of praises to the king.

In India there is a fruit, round as a calabash, which has three fruits inside, each with a different taste.

In India they worship the sun in a large temple outside of town. Every morning at sunrise the inhabitants rush out to this place and burn incense to a huge idol which, in a manner I cannot explain, turns around and makes a great noise.

In India they tell the future from the flight of birds.

In India if a man wants to burn himself alive, it is cause for great rejoicing. His family prepares a feast, then leads him on horse or on foot to the edge of a ditch. There he throws himself into the flames to the sound of music and celebration. Three days later he comes back to make his last will known; then he is gone forever.

In India it is very crowded because they have no pestilence. The number of people there exceeds belief. I saw armies of a million men or more.

It was so hot men's balls hung down to their knees, and the men had to tie them up and apply special ointments.

In India there is a bird called a *gookook* that flies in the night crying "gookook." Fire flashes from its beak. And if it lands on a roof, someone in that house will die that night.

In India they are much addicted to wantonness, but the unnatural crimes are unknown among them.

In India the dead are mourned for by women, who stand around the body, naked to the waist, and beat their breasts, crying "Alas! Alas!"

There is a race of barking people with the heads of dogs.

In India the ships are sewn like dresses, without a nail or a piece of iron in them, for there the rocks at sea draw iron to them, and any ship made with nails will crash against the rocks.

There is a race of horned people who grunt like pigs.

In India there are wells with hot water at night and cold during the day.

They clean their teeth with toothpicks.

In India the people are black. The blacker they are, the more beautiful they are thought to be. So every week they take their babies and rub them with oil till they become as black as devils. (Except that, in India, their gods are black and their devils white.)

In India each woman has many husbands, each with a specific duty. The wife lives in one house and her husbands in another. And they divide up the day so that each husband lives in his wife's house at certain hours, during which time no other husband may enter.

On one day of the year they light innumerable lamps of oil.

In India there are trees with leaves so big five or six men can stand in the shade of them.

They wash their feet first and then their faces. They wash before sleeping with their wives.

In India they worship the cow, and if one kills a cow he is immediately put to death. Some, particularly on holidays, even take the dung of the cow and rub it on their foreheads instead of perfume.

There are no adulterers there.

And I saw a temple high on a hill, and in it there was a single amethyst the size of a large pine cone, the color of fire, flashing from a distance as the sunbeams played about it.

In India there is a mountain called Albenigaras which is full of diamonds, but it swarms with venomous animals and serpents; no man can approach it. Next to it, however, is a higher mountain, and at certain times of the year the people climb it with oxen which they then cut to pieces. By means of machines they have invented, they throw the warm and bleeding hunks of meat below, onto the slopes of Albenigaras. Diamonds stick to the meat. Then vultures come and snatch the meat for food, flying off to places where they will be safe from the serpents. There the men go, and collect the diamonds that have fallen from the flesh.

In India the wise men can produce and quell great winds. For this reason they eat in secret.

In India the women wear wigs of black, the color they favor most. Some cover their heads with painted leaves, but none of them paint their faces.

There is a race of feathered people there who can leap into trees.

In India the men have no beards, but their hair is long and they tie it with a cord of silk and let it flow over their backs. In this way they go to war.

In India there is a fish whose skin is so hard that men make their houses out of it.

There is not a single tailor in India, for everyone goes naked.

In India it is very crowded, for the people are of a sort who are loathe to leave their own country.

In India they worship an idol, half man, half ox. And the idol speaks through its mouth and demands the blood of forty virgins. In one city I saw them carry their idol on a great chariot, and such was the fervor of the people that many cast themselves under the wheels of the chariot, that they may be crushed to death, as their god requires.

In India there is an animal called a *rhinoceros* because he has a horn over his nostril. And when he walks his horn jogs about, but when he becomes enraged by what he is looking at, his horn erects, and it becomes so rigid he can uproot a tree with it. His skin when it is dried is four fingers thick, and some people use it instead of iron for their plows, and they plow the earth with it.

There is a race of people there who are only one foot tall, and must always be on guard lest the storks carry them away. They are adult at age four and old men at eight.

In India there are roses everywhere—growing everywhere, for sale in the market, in wreaths around the necks of men and braided in the hair of the women. It seems they could hardly live without roses.

In India women sleep with their husbands in the day, but at night they go to foreign men and sleep with them and even pay them for it, for they like white people. And when a woman conceives a child by a stranger the husband pays him. If the child is born white the stranger receives eighteen tenkas extra; if it is black he gets nothing.

There is a race of people with backward feet.

In India there are long serpents called *cockodrilles* which live on land by day and in the water at night. In the winter they do not eat, but lie there dreaming. They kill men and devour them weeping.

In India there is a river known as the Arotani, where the fish are so abundant they can be caught by hand. But if anyone holds those fish in his hand for a short time he is immediately attacked by fever. As soon as he puts the fish down his health returns to him.

They use turbans for trousers.

They beat cymbals with a stick.

They kill their parents when they are old and use the flesh for food.

In India there is a tree, some three cubits high, which bears no fruit, and which is called, in their language, the tree of modesty. For if a man approaches it, it contracts and draws up all its branches, expanding again when he departs.

In India the girls have such firm flesh that you cannot squeeze it or pinch it anywhere. For a small coin they'll let a man pinch them as much as he likes. On account of this firmness, their breasts do not hang down at all, but stand straight out in front.

Peacocks run in the forest there.

And I saw a temple cast of solid bronze with an idol of solid gold the size of a man. Its eyes were made of two rubies, so skillfully done they seemed to be watching me.

They sit cross-legged on the ground.

In India the women go naked, and when a woman marries she is set on a horse, and her husband gets on the crupper and holds a knife pointed at her throat, and they both have nothing on except a tall cap on their heads like a miter, wrought with white flowers. And all the maidens of the place go singing in a row in front of them till they reach the house, and there the bride and groom are left alone, and when they get up in the morning they go as naked as before.

In India there are some who cut off their own heads, that they may go to Heaven. They use a strange sort of scissors.

In India if a man walks out of his house and hears someone

sneeze he immediately goes back inside and does not leave—for they think it is a bad omen.

There are people with ears like winnowing fans, and at night they lie on one and cover themselves with the other.

In India the men wear female dress; they use cosmetics, wear earrings, arm-rings, golden seal-rings on the ring finger as well as on the toes of the feet.

They eat alone, one by one, on a tablecloth of dung. After eating they throw the plates away.

They cohabit like a snake entwined by a vine, or rather, while their wives move back and forth as if they were plowing, the husbands remain motionless.

In India there is a bird called a *semenda* whose beak has several distinct pipes with many openings. When death approaches, this bird collects a quantity of dry wood in its nest, and sitting upon it, sings so sweetly with all its pipes that it attracts and soothes all listeners to a marvelous degree. Then, igniting the wood by flapping its wings, it allows itself to be burnt to death.

I asked them about their religion and they replied, "We believe in Adam."

In India the wife throws herself on her husband's funeral pyre, and if she will not do so, the people throw her there.

It was so hot swords melted in their scabbards, and the gems in their handles turned to coal.

There are headless men with eyes in their stomachs.

There are people who walk about on all fours.

In India there is a dragon called a *basilisk*, whose breath can pulverize a rock. Its tail can kill any animal except the elephant. It is said that when a man and a basilisk meet, if the creature sees the man first, the man dies; but if the man sees the basilisk first, then the creature will die.

In India when they dive for pearls they take their wise men with them, for the fish where the pearls are found are treacherous to man, but the wise men chant in such a way so as to stupefy the fish.

It is so cold that water turns to crystal, and on those crystals real diamonds grow. And the diamonds and the crystals mate and multiply and are nourished by the dew of heaven.

One morning a man of great stature and with a snowy white beard, naked from the waist up with only a mantle thrown about him and a knotted cord, appeared at my lodgings. He prostrated himself full length upon the sand, beating his head three times against the ground. Then he raised himself, and seeing my bare feet, wanted to kiss them, but I refused. And he told me that he came from an island across the sea, that he had been traveling for two years, and that he had come in search of me. For his attachment to his idols was so pure and devout that God had spoken to him, showed him my face, and told him to find me that he may be instructed in the true path.

There are warrior women with silver weapons, for they have no iron.

There are women with beards growing from their breasts.

And I saw, deep in the interior, Venetian ducats in circulation, and gold coins twice the size of our florins.

In India, they do not cut any hair of the body, not even the hair of the genitals, for they believe that cutting that hair increases carnal desire and incites to lust.

In India when they travel they like to have someone riding behind them.

In all emergencies they take the advice of women.

In India on one day of the year they set up poles like the masts of ships and hang from them pieces of beautiful cloth, interwoven with gold. On the top of each pole sits a man of pious aspect who prays for all. These men are assailed by the people, who pelt them with spoiled oranges, lemons, and other rank fruit, and the holy men must bear it all with equanimity.

In India when a child is born people show particular attention to the man, not to the woman. Of two children they give preference to the younger, for they maintain that the elder owes his birth to predominant lust, while the younger owes his origin to mature reflection and a calm proceeding.

There is a race of people there who have only one enormous foot, and when they want to rest in the noonday sun, they lie on their backs and raise their foot like a parasol. They are great runners.

In India they let their nails grow long, and glory in idleness.

There are little people who have no mouth, but only a small hole in their face, and they must suck their food through a straw.

In India they write the title of a book at the end.

And I saw one of their holy men, standing nude, facing the sun, cloaked with a panther skin, and I continued on my way. Sixteen years later I happened to return to the same place—and there he was, unmoved.

It was so hot fish at the bottom of the river burned like silk touched by a flame.

And I saw far off the coast of that land a thing in the sky, huge as a cloud, but black and moving faster than the clouds. I asked what that thing could be, and they said it is the great bird Rokh. But the wind was blowing off the coast, and the Rokh went with it, and I never got a closer look.

In India the birds and animals are completely different from ours, except for one: the quail.

[1984]

All of the imagery and some of the language are derived from works written in the five hundred years prior to 1492. India, of course, is where Columbus thought he was going.

Matteo Ricci

In the second half of the sixteenth century—after the conquest of the Americas—Madrid, Lisbon, and Rome were setting their sights on the material and ideological subjugation of the East. Portuguese beachheads had been established in Macao and Goa, and Francis Xavier himself had brought the Word to India and Japan. He died in 1552 on a barren island off the coast of China, trying to get in, dreaming of the conversion of the Ming Empire.

Goa, a tiny colony on a stretch of paradisaical beach, was a glimpse of the kind of world they might have made. It was a place where fortunes could be won, by whites, in the trade of cloth and spices, opium and kidnapped children. It was a place where Brahmins were sent to the galleys, temples razed, festivals and rites forbidden; where hundreds of schoolchildren would be assembled in rows to recite the Lord's Prayer and spit in unison at the mention of a Hindu god. In Goa, its Grand Inquisitor wrote, the land was "filled with fire and the ashes from the dead bodies of heretics and apostates." Their confiscated property was a useful source of income for the Church.

But the missionaries failed to penetrate deeper into India, failed even to interest, let alone convert the Mughal emperor, Akbar. Enthusiasm shifted to Japan, where they had, at first, greater success, but were soon disillusioned and defeated by the obscure motivations and the shifting alliances of the rival courts. China, under the rule of the weak Emperor Wanli, who rarely left the palace and allowed the country to be run by the eunuchs, then became the prize. The Jesuits in Macao had become rich from their investments in the Japan–China silk trade, which was monopolized by the Portuguese, and they had proved particularly helpful to the Chinese in the matter of returning slaves who had escaped from the interior into the colony. In 1582, thirty years after the death of Xavier, thanks to the familiar combination of bribery, favors, and coercion, they were permitted to take up residence in China itself.

They sent, among a few others, Matteo Ricci, who had spent five years in Goa and was to live for the next twenty-seven years, until his death, in China. He was, according to the historian Joseph Needham, "one of the most remarkable and brilliant men in history," and his residence, for good or ill, inserted China into the world. For the Chinese, Ricci was the bearer of the news of Western science; for the West, the posthumous publication of his journals and letters provided further tales of the wonders of China, a confirmation of Marco Polo who, after three hundred years, had receded into memory as a great fabulist.

There had been missionaries in China before: Nestorians from as early as the eighth century, and Franciscans in the thirteenth. All had failed and vanished. But Ricci succeeded by first establishing himself as a sage and a power broker, long before his purpose was made clear. He was, in a way, a mole for Jesus; he kept his crucifix hidden.

For the first six years he lived the role of a poor Buddhist monk, with shaved head and saffron robe, as he studied the language and the people, whom he thought would be drawn by his ascetic purity. The strategy failed, and he realized that he would attract attention only by being what he was, extraordinary. He switched to the elegant purple robes of a scholar and, with his new command of the language, found himself a celebrity.

He brought them clocks and astrolabes, harpsichords and telescopes. He translated Euclid and snatches of the Greek and Roman philosophers, wrote songs for the Emperor, calculated eclipses, reformed the calendar, prepared a map of the world with Chinese place-names, built sundials, and introduced Western theories and practices in hydraulics and surveying, geometry and optics, agriculture and astronomy.

He did not bring them, of course, the sciences themselves, but rather new information and new perspectives for re-evaluating what they already knew. For the Chinese scholars it was a return to the great age of Chinese science: a millennium or more that had ended, three centuries before, with the Mongol conquest.

And he did not bring them—except in small doses to the select few—the Christian dogma. He too dreamed of the conversion of China, and particularly hoped to win the Emperor Wanli. (The closest he came was being allowed—a great honor—to prostrate himself before the empty throne.) But he saw his primary function as that of establishing the respectability, and perhaps the superiority, of Western wisdom, thereby paving the way for the word of God. He was, he wrote, "opening up the wild woods and fighting with the wild beasts and poisonous snakes that lurk within."

He restricted his proselytizing to small gestures, like inscribing the sundials he built with homiletic messages on human frailty and God's grace. (As Cromwell's cannons were inscribed "God is Love.") The benign figure of Mary was emphasized to the point where the Chinese commonly believed the Christian God was a woman. When a palace eunuch discovered Ricci's crucifix, he thought it a black magic effigy in a plot to kill the emperor. (Indeed, one wonders how the missionaries ever hoped to replace the image of the beatific Buddha with that of a man undergoing torture.) In general, the Chinese thought he was an alchemist, and confused him with the Muslims, Jews, and Nestorian Christians who had passed through the country. They saw no distinctions between the three Mediterranean monotheisms, and in that they may have been wiser than the West.

In the spiritual woods of China, there is no doubt that Ricci thought himself among "wild beasts and poisonous snakes." He assumed that Asians were "born to serve rather than command," and had no qualms about slavery. (In fact, he believed it to be one of God's ways of bringing in converts, and owned a few himself.) He misread Confucian doctrine, with its hierarchy leading up to a supreme ruler, as a rudimentary form of monotheism, and thought it had "the fewest errors of all pagan sects." Buddhism he found "a Babylon"—a seething fleshpot—"of doctrines." Converts—and there were not, at first, very many—were praised for destroying their heathen sculpture and books.

Yet what was extraordinary, almost sinister, about Ricci was his tremendous understanding of Chinese things, a sympathy within the antipathy (or perhaps vice versa). His Christian writings in Chinese sound like something from the Four Classics: "A man who has strong faith in the Way can walk on the yielding water as if on solid rock . . . When the wise man follows heaven's decrees, fire does not burn him, a sword does not cut him, water does not drown him.'' And his marvelous map of the world presents the six continents (Europe, Libya, Asia, North America, South America, and Mowalanichia, that great mass south of the capes of Good Hope and the Horn) in the loopy Swiss-cheese style of esoteric Taoist art, where the solid is defined by the void, the earth by the "constellation holes" of the sky. Sinophile and Sinophobe, inexhaustible fountain of information about both East and West, he worked in tremendous isolation. Letters from Europe could take seventeen years to arrive (three was the norm) and most of Ricci's library was carried in his head.

His prodigious memory was the product of intensive mnemonic training in the Jesuit colleges of Rome and Florence, where he learned a system of memory techniques that dated back at least to the first century B.C. and was to last until cheap printing simplified access to information. [Francis Yates' great book, *The Art of Memory*, details its history as an organizing principle for much of Medieval and Renaissance culture.] In a world where most memories are stored outside the brain, the system seems impossible today: it depended on the construction of imaginary mental palaces, its rooms filled with bric-a-brac of indelible, highly associative images.

Ricci's first book in Chinese was a *Treatise on Friendship*—a nice gesture. His second was a *Treatise on the Mnemonic Arts*, which he correctly guessed would draw the young men who needed to memorize the classics in order to pass the examinations that ensured a place in the bureaucracy. (The Chinese mnemonic system, which had produced wonders, had by that time largely disappeared and is now unknown.)

That memory book has, four hundred years later, spun into another book, a biography by the Sinologist Jonathan Spence, called *The Memory Palace of Matteo Ricci*. What is remarkable is that Spence has allowed the mnemonic system to direct the course of his work. He takes four images from Ricci's *Treatise*, as well as four Bible illustrations which Ricci provided for a print-maker as examples of Western art, and lets each of the images lead him to a topic: war and violence, water and travel, foreigners, trade and profit, understanding and education, sin, the Virgin Mary. These are discussed without chronological sequence; the action shifts back and forth between Asia and the Europe of the Counter Reformation, between historical and biographical events.

It is a dazzling structure for a Western biography: to take a word like "water," and then extrapolate, in meticulous detail, what it would have meant to this person, living in this time and these places. But it is not that unusual for the East. Perhaps the most beautiful autobiography in Chinese, Shen Fu's *Six Records of A Floating Life* (1809), is organized by emotion: the delights of travel, the sorrows of misfortune, the pleasures of leisure. Chronological time does not exist: Shen Fu tosses off sentences like "Yun [his wife] had given birth to a girl named Jing-jun, who by then was fourteen years old." [Sixty years later, Flaubert would create a scandal by collapsing sixteen years of Frédéric Moreau's life into the words "He traveled."] But Shen Fu's book is heavy with time: memory-time, nostalgia, a time where everything is in the past tense, where every event, as soon as it is recalled, recalls its outcome.

The Western technique of the flashback is essentially an artificial rearrangement of chronological sequences; it is not memory-time. The memory thinks simultaneously of beginning, middle, and end; its sense of time is only the loss of time. Wordsworth and Proust, in their searches for lost time, assume that memory is a stream, a stream they follow against its current. But the memory is a vortex, a simultaneity. [And *vortex* is an East-West conjunction: Pound found the term in the pamphlets on Hinduism he read in his late adolescence.] No matter what the subject, the memory always thinks of something else, is always creating still lifes, collages. The pure (impossible) biography or autobiography would create constellations out of one mind's associations, distractions, incongruous leaps; it would be regardless of time.

What Spence has attempted is a psychohistory that ignores most of twentieth-century psychology, which is dependent on narrative, flashback, cause and effect. His Ricci is not the result of obsessions and repressions, cruel or benevolent parents, time bombs planted in childhood, but rather the sum of his mental (and not particularly emotive) associations; a Ricci inseparable from his mnemonic system. It is, curiously, Matteo Ricci as Jorge

Luis Borges. Not Borges the man, but Borges the character created by Borges: the man of pure memory, whose head is simultaneously library and labyrinth, a vast library whose arrangement can only partially be deciphered.

This model of library and labyrinth has become scientific: It is now thought that the brain is indeed organized topically. [In one recent case, a man who had suffered a head injury could not recall—and when reminded could not retain—the names of any fruits or vegetables; his memory was otherwise intact.] Yet each topic resides in a room with a million doors; each door leading instantly to another room, another topic, and then another. In Ricci's time, apparently, it was possible to map out this infinite palace of rooms, even to organize its interior decoration. In the twentieth century it has come to resemble the mansion of Citizen Kane. Our metaphor for memory is the modernist poem; and in its collages, mental shorthand, even in its incomprehensible passages, it may be the purest form of autobiography: the text closest to its inventing mind.

[1984]

Falkland Road

The three worlds (Sky-Air-Earth) were united; the gods divided them into three. The worlds grieved that they had been divided in three, and the gods said, "Let us take the three sorrows from these three worlds." Indra removed their sorrow, and the grief which the god removed from this earth entered the whore; the grief which god removed from the air entered the eunuch; the grief from heaven entered the sinful man or the rogue.

—The Brāhmanas

Falkland Road, in the Kamathipura section, is the red-light district for the working class in Bombay. It is within walking distance of two other flumes of the city, one turbulent, one almost still: Bombay Central, the railroad station for millions, communal home for thousands, antheap and inevitable sluicegate in the endless flow of pilgrimages, business trips, and family visits that is Indian life; and the Towers of Silence, forbidden both to passers-by and to the faithful, where the Parsis leave their dead to be eaten by vultures, so that water, earth, and fire remain undefiled by corpses. The three form a delta of passage: passion, pilgrimage, death. A mirror to India's spiritual non-passages: the sex without orgasm of Tantrism, the motionless pilgrimage of Yoga, and the release from the cycle of death and rebirth of Buddhism.

Falkland Road, like everything in India, is compartmentalized and arranged vertically and horizontally. Like red-light districts everywhere, it is both an epitome and a parody of the society in which it exists. At the bottom are the "cage girls": bizarrely made-up and dressed, they stand at street level in a barred version of the Indian shop, lifting their skirts and shouting obscenities at the men in the street. Despised by other prostitutes, they are the cheapest tricks (about thirty cents) and a grotesque caricature of the Indian woman as an immobile commodity and object of desire. Their opposites on the bottom rung are the street girls (and *girls* is the word—the workers of Falkland Road are mainly young teenagers): independents, tied to no brothel, who find their own customers in the cafés, work in hired rooms, and sleep in the streets. Mistrusted by the other prostitutes for their freedom and self-reliance, their very mobility is a negation of the traditional Indian woman and her parody, the cage girl.

Above the street are the brothels, where the girls are among the last in India to live in a strict version of *purdah*. They rarely go out and are rigidly controlled—but also protected and literally blessed daily—by their madams. They are more conservatively dressed than the cage girls; they could pass unnoticed in a crowd, except, perhaps, for their beauty. As the *purdah* system collapses in modern India, it is curious that these last sequestered women are the ones most accessible to men. As so often happens, the structure remains, in contradiction to its original function.

Parallel to the female brothels are those of the *hinjras*, who work both in cages and in the rooms above. They are the most mysterious caste in North India: transvestites, some of them eunuchs, who dance at festivals, and at weddings and funerals. They play the role of Fool, object of derision, the chaos that reaffirms the order of "normal" society; but also, strangely, they are images of the cosmic androgyny, the oneness of the universe. Their ranks are replenished by abandoned and, some say, kidnapped infants and boys. Their main source of income is prostitution; their clients homosexual men.

Falkland Road seems largely unchanged since the last major report to the West of its activities: Alfred Dyer's dispatches to the English papers in 1887. But there is one difference: a hundred years ago, the workers and customers on the street were interracial. (And, interestingly, the white women were almost all Jews who had fled the persecution in Eastern Europe.) Today Falkland Road is an entirely Indian institution.

Current news of the district has arrived in the unlikely form of *Falkland Road*, an elegant book of photographs with a short text, both by Mary Ellen Mark. A well-known Magnum photographer, Mark "had thought about Falkland Road for ten years," but her early attempts at taking pictures there had been frustrated. Crowds of men gathered around, and the prostitutes threw water and garbage on her from the windows above—as they had done, a hundred years earlier, on members of the Bombay Midnight Mission. She writes, in perhaps the most revealing moment of the book:

> In October of 1978 I decided to return to Bombay and try somehow to enter the world of these women and to photograph them. I had no idea if I could do this. But I knew I had to try. The night before I left I had a vivid dream: I was a voyeur hiding behind a bed in a brothel on Falkland Road watching three transvestite prostitutes making love. I awoke amused and somewhat reassured. Perhaps my dream was a good sign.

By her own standards, Mark succeeded: an expensive book was produced by Knopf, and has become something of a commercial success. But what is one to make of this success, and of this dream that hangs over the chasm between Falkland Road and *Falkland Road*?

Photography began with the transformation of the familiar into the exotic. The first photographs were of ourselves and of local sights. The self became the other: one sat motionless for twenty minutes for a daguerreotype not to see oneself, but to see how one looked in a photograph, to see another image of the self. (And later, time would add a second layer of exoticism: the strangeness we all feel, looking at old snapshots of ourselves.) It was, in the anonymity of the industrial cities, a beginning of self-consciousness, alienated "modern" man.

But photography, after the initial amazement, quickly assumed a more important role: the transformation of the exotic into the familiar. Not only did everything in the world exist to end up in a photograph (as Sontag writes, via Mallarmé) but the world itself seemed a bundle of gathered photographic images. Photography became a form of both tourism and colonialism. Its rise, not coincidentally, is parallel to that of the great capitalist empires.

This tourism was always vertical and horizontal. Horizontal: to the ends of the earth, where the new photographer-adventurers traveled to supply the inexhaustible demand for fresh "views." And vertical (though mainly downward): epitomized by the title of Jacob Riis' classic 1890 study of the New York poor, *How the Other Half Lives*. Today, the search for new images of horizontal tourism has played out: we know what most of the world looks like in a photograph, are bored by friends' snapshots of Urumqi or Baffin Island, and will buy a book of "travel photographs" only if the photographer is extraordinary. But vertical photographic tourism is flourishing, now more than ever. Middle-class curiosity about the fringes of society seems insatiable, and the collection of these images has become a small industry for the leagues of "photojournalists": talented workers, like Mark, who lack the transformative vision of the great "fine art" photographers. In recent years there have been books of photos of wrestlers, strippers, tattooed people, body-builders, transvestites, junkies, shopping-bag ladies, mental patients (including Mark's own *Ward 81*) and various groups of urban and rural poor—to name only a few—but none of typists, management consultants, philatelists, Sunday golfers. Like the Romans pouring fish emulsion over their food—to bring a little taste to a palate deadened by the lead from their water pipes and goblets—the audience has become numb to images of the ordinary world. To get high, it needs an increasingly stronger fix of the strange. (Or, at the least, demands that the ordinary be made to look strange.)

Daguerre believed he had "made a window men look through," much as Whitman wanted to create "a perfectly transparent plate-glass style." Both of course were wrong: a photograph, no less than a poem, is a metaphor, not the world. The camera, not the print, is the window. Photographs, as Ansel Adams' formula goes, are made and not taken (and in fact much of the work takes place in the darkroom; its procedures, and ultimate appreciation, are not all that different from those of painting). And yet the act of photography, the moment of pressing the shutter, may be the only new development in creative composition since Lascaux.

It is an immediate act, without recollection, absorption, trans-

formation, revision; it is an action painting produced in a split
second. And it is an act of immediate power. The camera is a
weapon, its language ballistic. With a camera or a rifle, as any
tourist or terrorist knows, one can get a stranger or a crowd of
strangers to do almost anything. But the camera is also a window: the photographer always stands removed from the action,
whether or not it is under her or his direction. In the familiar
disaster scenario, the photographer shoots first, then aids the
victim, if at all.

To stand at the window watching, like Tonio Kroger, like
Proust, has been a frequent metaphor for the artist. With photography, the metaphor becomes actual practice. To photograph is
have the Superman x-ray vision of childhood fantasy: everything
is made visible, but from afar. It is to collect as many images as
possible from a world one sometimes controls, but does not
participate in. It is to dream that one is a voyeur, watching three
eunuchs fuck in a run-down Bombay brothel, and to wake, not
appalled, but refreshed.

Here then is this object, *Falkland Road*. In many ways it is a
book told by its cover: a frame with gold letters on a rich maroon;
within the frame a portrait of an extraordinarily beautiful
woman, seen nude from the waist up, wearing only an ornate
necklace. It is a photograph from a fashion magazine: the woman
is breathtaking but vacuous; she stares at the camera and at us
with a model's haughtiness and hostility; nothing is revealed.
Only inside the book do we learn that her name is Putla (an eerie
resemblance to the Spanish *puta*), that she is thirteen years old,
that she was sold to the brothel at twelve, that her madam
complains that it took four months to "break her in." The
contrast of image and caption is not intentionally ironic: it is the
distance between photographer and subject—the distance that
occurs when content is dissolved by style.

In sixty-five photographs, shot in deep but often murky color,
we see the women and transvestites washing, waiting, clowning,
posing, nursing their babies, dressing, cleaning their rooms and,
amazingly, working. With the exception of the latter, these are
fairly ordinary photographs of ordinary activities, given interest
only because we know who these people are, at least profession-

ally. Many of the pictures are characterized by that peculiarly Indian *stare*. The camera is still a novelty in the country, and many photographers and filmmakers have found inescapable that look of blank curiosity, fear, and impossible distance. In India, it is the subject, not the photographer, who sees more intensely.

In these photographs we always sense Mark as an outsider, not in the tension of a cultural clash that might have produced more interesting work, but rather a simple and numb remoteness. The effect is disturbing: the prostitute, the extreme example of person as sex item, is even further objectified. [The comparison is somewhat unfair, but many will automatically think of the photographs taken by E. J. Bellocq in the Storyville section of New Orleans at the turn of the century. Bellocq, a hydrocephalic dwarf, befriended—and never hired—the prostitutes; his photographs, a dialogue between outcasts, remain among the most loving portraits of women. Although nothing is known of these women—and little of Bellocq himself—no captions are necessary: Storyville lives in a way that Falkland Road, despite Mark's claim of love and friendship for these "special women," never does. And Bellocq, of course, would never have used the phrase "special women."]

What are remarkable, however, are the working pictures. They are probably the first non-pornographic representations of Indian sex since the last of the great miniature paintings in the ninteenth century. Prostitutes have long served as nude models for painting and photography—they are, after all, accustomed to being undressed objects—but it is surprising that Mark was also able to persuade the johns to pose, and in action. And it is the presence of the johns that gives us our only glimpse of how squalid life on Falkland Road is: though the women all have a natural dignity and occasionally beauty, the johns are unrelievedly sleazy.

The sex, on bare mattresses in tiny cubicles, is mainly depressing: we are centuries away from the exuberance of Indian erotic art. (And, also from its variety: according to an interview with Mark, the sex is all "straight fucking"; the thousand pretzel positions that India invented have, at least on Falkland Road, unraveled to one.) In the saddest picture in the book, a man, still wearing his gaudy shirt, lies on top of a young woman who stares at us with a resigned and vacant melancholy. The camera's perspective is that of Kali, goddess of annihilation, looking down as she stands on the back of Rati, who copulates with Kama in the familiar miniature scene. But this girl's name is Kamla, not Kama, and she speaks in the caption: "Often when I am with a customer, I hold my legs straight and he doesn't even enter me. After all, my body is my own." Kama and Rati were symbols of the desire that created the universe; in Kamla's eyes it is, almost, the end of the world.

Falkland Road is a piece of the world that few of us could stand for more than a few minutes. Yet packaged as *Falkland Road* it is an object with some popular appeal, though it is neither pornography nor reformist exposé. Its attraction, as far as I can tell, is its double dream: First, the dream of travel and its unchanging equation of exotic and erotic: sex, as we all know, is always more available, and wilder, someplace else. Second, the dream of the photograph: to see everything in the world—at a safe distance. These dreams are so powerful that they obscure the dreary evidence of the photographs themselves. Who can resist these images of "real" people fucking in some strange corner of the earth? It is like watching firemen battle a blaze around the corner, knowing that one's own house is safe.

[1981]

The News from Naropa

"To cling to sectarian bigotry and dogma
makes one vicious . . ."
—Milarepa

1

Though local variants may add or subtract a few details, though
some tellings are terrifying and some comical, the story of the
Spiritual Leader and his Organization may be the most familiar
tale of the last decade. In this version from Boulder, Colorado,
the protagonist sits on a small throne in a business suit, or is
chauffeured about in a Mercedes limo, always accompanied by a
retinue of guards. He is a chain smoker, an alcoholic who becomes carried away at parties, and often must be carried away
from parties. An ardent anti-Communist, a supporter of Nixon
in 1972 and Ford in 1976, he dismisses all other religions and
spiritual disciplines. It is said that he orders his disciples to beat
each other and to sleep with each other; that he himself beats
some and sleeps with more than some. His favorite metaphor for
himself is that of a doctor who operates without anaethesia. His
disciples work as the unpaid servants in his mansion, dress in
formal attire, and call him "Your Highness."

His Organization has millions of dollars of real estate across
the country, spiritual centers built by volunteer disciple labor,
and a "secular" educational institution. Fortunes are paid to
professional public relations consultants while students and
disciples are dunned for more cash. The standard dress is the
three-piece suit; business activities, hard drinking, and sexual
promiscuity are apparently encouraged. Critics are physically
threatened; unfavorable published opinion is obliterated as

members buy all the copies off the stands. The disciples' favorite metaphor for themselves is "warrior"; competition among them is fierce. The word that most often tumbles from their mouths is "paranoia."

The tale has become commonplace these days, but in this version the cast of characters is unique and disturbing, for the Spiritual Leader is Chogyam Trungpa, Rinpoche; his best-known follower is Allen Ginsberg; and those who have taught under his auspices include many of the best writers, artists, composers, and academics in the land. Whereas most of the recent crackpot pantheons can be shrugged off as cults appealing only to dopes and the doped, the tale of Trungpa is difficult to ignore. What is happening in Boulder, in an embryonic form, seems to be an Oriental redecoration of home-grown American fascism: the Dharma Bums playing *It Can't Happen Here*. And as George Orwell wrote in 1946, "A writer's political and religious beliefs are not excrescences to be laughed away, but something that will leave their mark even on the smallest details of his work."

Trungpa, whatever his excesses, is no imposter. His lineage is that of the Kagyupa and Karmapa orders, both founded by disciples of the great Milarepa (1040–1123) to carry on the Nyingmapa tradition. [The Nyingmapa is the "ancient" or "unreformed" school, which emphasizes "action," principally meditation. Its complement is the Gelukpa or "reformed" school, stressing scholarship; it is now the dominant order, headed by the Dalai Lama.] The Karmapa order initiated the system of succession by reincarnation, later adopted by the other orders. Chogyam Trungpa, born (or rather reborn) in 1938, was discovered as an infant to be the eleventh incarnation of Trungpa Tulku. From age two he was raised to be the Supreme Abbot of the Sumang monasteries in eastern Tibet.

Following the Chinese takeover of Tibet in 1959, Trungpa fled to India. Four years later he went to England, possibly with CIA help, to study at Oxford. After graduation he founded, in Scotland, the first Tibetan Buddhist meditation center in the West, Samye-Ling. Here was his first encounter with American poetry, in the figure of the redoubtable Robert Bly, who came to study and later helped Trungpa edit his lectures for English publication. Trungpa became the first Tibetan to obtain British citizenship (which he retains) and shortly thereafter he renounced his monastic vows to marry a wealthy sixteen-year-old disciple. Though marriage is not unknown among the lesser monks in Trungpa's order, his peers and disciples were unhappy with a connubial version of the Master's Bliss, and the newlyweds soon left Scotland for—where else?—the United States.

In Vermont in 1970 he founded America's first Tibetan meditation center, called Tail of the Tiger. Trungpa was quick to master the Way of America: Tail of the Tiger (with property and buildings worth a million dollars) was followed by large purchases of land in eight other states, a Mudra Theater Group, a Maitri Therapy Project, and various publishing ventures which made Trungpa's writings bestsellers on the spiritual circuit. In 1973 he inaugurated the Vajradhatu Seminary, three months of intensive retreat at resorts featuring Tibetan-style scenery. The first Seminary, at Jackson Hole, included Allen Ginsberg among its students.

Through Ginsberg, Bly, and others, Trungpa had become the pet guru of many poets. (He was, after all, Oxford-educated and something of a poet himself.) In 1974, taking advantage of his literary conquests, he founded the Naropa Institute in Boulder, Colorado, a parochial but eclectic college. Naropa's best-known department, initiated the same summer, was the Jack Kerouac School of Disembodied Poetics, under the leadership of Ginsberg and Anne Waldman. Their aim was a reincarnation in the lineage of Black Mountain and the Bauhaus, and Naropa attracted a galaxy of artists—Ashbery, Burroughs, Creeley, Dorn, Corso, DiPrima, Cage, Don Cherry, Baraka, McClure, Duncan, Berrigan, Whalen, Rakosi, Tarn, Merwin, Sanders, Rothenberg, Joni Mitchell—most of whom were Ginsberg connections rather than Trungpa disciples.

Trungpa's relations with these artists seemed, from the beginning, mixed: on the one hand, elation at having the all-stars on his team; on the other, what insiders would call his scorn of the artist's self-involvement, and outsiders might see as envy or fear of eclipse. The first sign of trouble had occurred in 1972, at a benefit reading for Trungpa given by Ginsberg, Bly, and Gary Snyder. Trungpa, completely drunk, trashed the event: banging on a gong, interrupting the readings, ridiculing the poets. Bly never forgave him; Snyder thereafter made himself scarce; and only Ginsberg humbly swallowed Trungpa's explanation (Ginsberg: "Your drunken behavior—is this just you, or is this a traditional manner, or what?" Trungpa: "I come from a long line of eccentric Buddhists.") and subsequently defended his teacher to all and sundry.

The major incident, however, the Lexington & Concord of what became a spiritual-literary war, took place in 1975 at a Halloween party at the Vajradhatu Seminary in Snowmass, Colorado. The story has taken on an almost legendary status, but it is possible to separate the facts from the oral embellishments by reading *The Party* ("a chronological perspective on a confrontation at a Buddhist seminary, prepared and written by members of the Investigative Poetry Group under the direction of Ed Sanders, investigative coordinator") which devotes about a hundred pages to documentation of the event. The incident itself is more emblematic than definitive, and the response to it far more interesting than the episode itself.

Briefly then, the story: In 1975, W. S. Merwin was teaching a summer course at Naropa, and he asked Trungpa if he and his companion, the Hawaiian poet Dana Naone, could attend the Vajradhatu Seminary in the fall. Though Merwin and Naone were considered beginners, and the Seminary was strictly for advanced and favored students (competition for admittance was keen) Trungpa accepted—possibly because Merwin was, next to Ginsberg, his choicest poetry catch. At the Seminary Merwin and Naone participated in all the activities, but generally kept to themselves—a source of resentment in a community devoted to the dissolution of the self. After two thirds of the teachings had been completed, and the "powerful stuff" (Vajrayana, the Tantric teachings) was about to begin, Trungpa declared a costume party for Halloween night.

It was a wild party: Trungpa, smashed, necking with a disciple and leaving teeth marks on her cheek, ordering his guards to strip a sixty-year-old woman and carry her around the room, and other scenes of merriment. Merwin and Naone, in no mood for bacchanalia, had come and left. Somewhere in his haze the Leader noted the absence of the prize pupil; the guards were told to summon

them from their room. Merwin and Naone replied that they were
tired, were going to bed. Trungpa ordered them to appear. Tension escalated. Merwin and Naone, terrified, barricaded their
door with furniture. Trungpa demanded the door be broken
down. The faithful climbed over a balcony and smashed through
plate-glass doors; Merwin, though a lifelong pacifist, began slash-
ing wildly with a broken beer bottle. But at the sight of blood—
several attackers were seriously hurt—he stopped, and the pair
allowed themselves to be taken to the party.

Confronting Trungpa, he answered their objections by throwing saké in Merwin's face and making remarks to Naone insinuating his displeasure that a fellow Asian would consort with a
white man. He then ordered his guards to strip both of them. As
Naone screamed for help a hundred disciples stood and watched
in silence. Only one, named Bill King, tried to intervene;
Trungpa punched him in the face and the guards dragged him
out. Finally the poets stood, naked and huddling, before the
Leader. In a pathetic moment, Naone had cried "Call the police!" as if the outside world still existed. (Ginsberg was later to
comment: "In the middle of that scene, to yell 'call the police'—
do you realize how *vulgar* that was? The Wisdom of the East was
being unveiled, and she's going 'call the police!' I mean, shit!
Fuck that shit! Strip 'em naked, break down the door!") The next
morning Trungpa placed this letter in the disciples' mailboxes—
a classic of Orientalist Americana, spiritual doubletalk and the
inevitable financial considerations:

Dear friends,

In order to present comprehensive communication between the students and myself, I have come to the conclusion that we need to
break the ice of our personal concealment. It is time for us all to be
honest. If you want to maintain your patterns of hiding your deception, you are invited to leave the seminary before the vajrayana
teachings begin. Since your neurosis is already an open secret, you
could be braver in unmasking it. Without commitment to yourself,
there is no ground to present the vajrayana teachings to you. I in-
vite you to be yourself, without trips. I would like to encourage you
to make a proper relationship to the coming vajrayana talks. This
requires of you the understanding that we are not fooling each
other. Since you are all pretty involved in the teachings, your at-

tempt at deception is a useless hesitation. In order to recognize your personal deceit, you must understand the umbilical cord between you and me. You must offer your neurosis as a feast to celebrate your entrance into the vajra teachings. Those of you who wish to leave will not be given a refund, but your karmic debt will continue as the vividness of your memory cannot be forgotten.

Chogyam Trungpa, the Venerable Vajra
Chogyam Trungpa, Rinpoche

The tale of Merwin, Naone, and Trungpa quickly became myth, and its archetypal qualities have kept the myth not only alive, but perhaps more vivid than ever now, several years later. Here was the mad king, the mob beyond the barricaded door, the thugs smashing through the glass, the pacifist turned enraged protector, the triumph of the sinister, the group apathy to violence, and finally—as Robert Duncan has pointed out—the nude heterosexual couple as emblems of resistance. It is the stuff of nightmares, complete with its ideologies: fascism, sexism, racism. Trungpa calls his teachings "crazy wisdom"—was it crazy or was it wisdom, a method or madness?

In the literary world, repercussions were felt almost immediately. Robert Bly was telling his reading audiences a characteristically garbled version of the event, and word reached the National Endowment for the Arts, then considering a grant application from the Kerouac School. Ginsberg and Anne Waldman scrambled to disassociate Naropa from the Vajradhatu Seminary,* to have the NEA talk to Merwin, Bly, anybody. The application was turned down. Trungpa's private secretary circulated a letter warning disciples of the "enemies of the dharma."

---

*Disciples claim that Naropa is not parochial, and is completely separate from the Vajradhatu organization. Naropa is a division of the Nalanda Foundation, and is indeed *legally* separate from Vajradhatu—a common bureaucratic arrangement for tax and grant purposes. However, Trungpa is the president (with veto power) of both organizations and, at the time of the Sanders report, all six directors of Vajradhatu were directors of Nalanda, and all six officers of Nalanda were officers of Vajradhatu. There is no question that Naropa is a Buddhist institution: it is plain in all their brochures and catalogs. Meditation is "highly encouraged" and may soon be required in their new degree program; the administration consists largely of Trungpa disciples, and Trungpa himself has stated that "the purpose of Naropa is, first of all, to provide a vessel for the development of Boddhisattva activity."

Then in 1977 Ed Sanders was invited to teach a summer course at Naropa. His subject was "Investigative Poetics," a Sanders invention which proclaims that "poetry should again assume responsibility for the description of history." He asked his class which topic they wished to explore, and they chose, of course, the Merwin incident. Naropa—reminiscent of the last months of the Nixon administration—made no attempt to stop the investigation. The twenty students interviewed some sixty people, not including Trungpa himself, who refused to cooperate. Merwin and Naone, then in France, sent a long letter—their only public comments to date. The final report, *The Party*, is 178 pages long and covers the 1972 Bly-Ginsberg-Snyder reading, various Seminary brawls, the Halloween party, Bly's subsequent statements, and the NEA rhubarb. It is brilliantly edited, a fascinating narrative: the same story told over and over, detail by detail, with contradictions, additions, lacunae, and wonderful bits of spiritual Newspeak, such as "Merwin and Dana were overcompensating physically."

In 1978 *The Party* began circulating in samizdat, despite various attempts to suppress it. The copy I received had a xeroxed letter on the first page which reads:

Dear [blacked out],

I am sending you my copy of Ed Sander's piece on the W. S. Merwin affair. [Blacked out] has asked me to entrust this copy with you.

[Paragraph blacked out]

I would also ask that you not mention from whom you received this report. It may be paranoid, but in light of the threats that Clark and Dorn have received, I would rather remain anonymous.

Sincerely,
[Blacked out]

The controversy, though three years old, was intensifying as the report found new readers. The response from the Naropa and Vajradhatu community was entrenchment, fear, petty and serious counterattack, and a kind of madness.

Evidence of the hysterical mood then prevalent comes from a

source unrelated to the Merwin story. As documented in the July 1979 issue of *Tibetan Review* (under the title "The Nadir of Sectarian Squabbles?") it seems that in late November 1978 (coincident to the Jonestown suicides) Karl G. Springer, Director for External Affairs of Vajradhatu, circulated a letter to all U.S. members claiming that the Dalai Lama was plotting the assassination of the Gyalwa Karmapa (the main man in Trungpa's line) and other high Nyingmapa lamas. He further charged that the Dalai Lama was "de-emphasizing" Buddhism in an attempt to effect rapprochement with the Chinese, and that Nyingmapa spirituality was therefore an obstacle to the plan.* The letter orders all of the Dharmadhatu centers (i.e., the local branches) to meet immediately to discuss the situation, and to send letters (all with an identical text, supplied by Springer) to the Indian and Sikkimese governments demanding police protection for the lamas.

Springer was clearly not acting on his own: such a charge could have come only with Trungpa's crazy blessing, if not under his direct orders. As might be expected, Springer's letter provoked vehement responses from various lamas, not only calling the whole plot absurd, but pointing out that Springer was absolutely incorrect in even the tiniest details of his report. Half a year later, after the rumor was firmly planted, Springer half-heartedly apologized. A few months after that, the Dalai Lama, on his first visit to the U.S., canceled a scheduled stop at Boulder. It is now said that the Springer affair has alienated Trungpa from other important lamas in the U.S. and that even the Karmapa is extremely displeased by the tales of Trungpa's activities in bed and with bottle. [This is, of course, difficult to verify, but one small clue is provided by an issue of *The Tibet Journal* devoted to the Dalai Lama's 1979 trip to the U.S. In two dozen photographs, the Dalai Lama is seen shaking hands with, or standing next to, various dignitaries. In the photograph of Trungpa's meeting with the Dalai Lama in New York, however, Trungpa is bowing to his

---

*This probably needs some translating. Imagine, then, a high-ranking official of the Anglican Church sending a letter to every parish in England stating that the Pope is planning to bump off the Archbishop of Canterbury in order to foster relations with the Soviet Union by weakening European Christianity.

superior. *The Tibet Journal* is an official publication from Dharamsala, the Dalai Lama's capital-in-exile. That Trungpa alone is shown in a position of fealty is hardly accidental in a tradition where hierarchical gestures are tremendously important.]

Hangovers from the party continued through 1979. In February, *Harper's* published "Spiritual Obedience" (the title tells all) by Peter Marin, a diary of a summer at Naropa, and the first national account of the Merwin story, although Marin, oddly, uses no names. In March, *Boulder Monthly* published an excerpt from the Sanders report, accompanied by Tom Clark's interview with Ginsberg on the incident. (The Naropans formed squads and bought up every copy.) This was followed by a petition, circulated by Bob Callahan of Turtle Island Press, calling for a boycott of Naropa. The petition was a flop: even those who loathed Trungpa refused to attack Ginsberg's baby. According to Callahan, "It was a case of party lines, party loyalty, of not losing gigs or giving up a station."

Flak flew throughout the year, culminating in the publication of Tom Clark's book, *The Great Naropa Poetry Wars*, the first published history of the controversy, but one unfortunately full of wild rumors dropped in wiseacre style. To date, Trungpa has made no public statements on the incident, and Ginsberg continues his private lobbying.

2

The Kingdom of Prester John, Eden itself: the spiritual paradises invented by the West have all been somewhere in Asia (the material paradises were in the New World). The last of them was, until recently, Tibet. [Immanuel Kant: "This is the highest country; no doubt it was inhabited before any other and could even have been the site of all creation and science. The culture of the Indians, as is known, almost certainly came from Tibet, just as all our arts like agriculture, numbers, the game of chess, etc. seem to have come from India."]

Tibet: a Shangri-la of other-worldliness, of chants and strange music echoing in the mountains, meditation, telepathy, astral projection. Perhaps it all did indeed exist there, but religion, everywhere, is primarily concerned with power—the sources and manifestations of power. Divine power has inevitably become entwined with worldly power; there has never been an apolitical religion. (Even the wandering mendicant is, in himself, a criticism of the existing political structure.) The actual history of Tibet is as violent and depressing as any other history: the continual rise and fall of warring monasteries and sects, each connected to a noble family; the forging and breaking of alliances; endless vendettas; holy squanderers supported by a miserable majority of landless serfs—and a few great teachers, criticizing and struggling against the worldly excesses of their contemporaries. Tibet until 1959 is the mirror of medieval Europe, its Buddhism a rigid and hierarchical institution whose relation to the teachings of the Gautama corresponds to that between the medieval papacy and the guru from Nazareth.

Tibetan Buddhism and the medieval Church: both are defined by the magnificence of their scholarship and art, their legends of exemplary men, and the local anecdotes of sex, greed, exploitation, and debauchery. In both cultures the lusty monk is a stock comic figure among the common people. In both, the advocates of reform are swallowed by the institution. This is the tradition Trungpa comes from. If we ignore the exoticism of his Eastern trappings, we might imagine him as a bishop who walked out of a time warp, discoursing brilliantly on Aquinas and Augustine while peddling papal indulgences.

Not only has Trungpa walked out of a medieval theocracy into a land full of spiritual junk food, he also comes from a tradition where the teachings are largely transmitted orally—for though Tibetan Buddhism has produced a sea of books, these are mainly mnemonic devices, touchstones, starting points for pedagogical exegesis. The heart of the religion then, especially in the "active" Nyingmapa tradition, becomes the relation between master and disciple. The typical Christian tale is of miracles and torture; in Tibet, the stories of the saints usually concern the ordeals imposed by the teacher on his student: impossible and useless tasks, senseless beatings—a kind of physical version of the Zen koan, designed to stop the flow of discursive thought in the disciple's mind, allowing him to project outside of the self. Even debates between lamas of equal rank become a physical combat: early

travelers to Tibet were startled by these formal contests where
points were made with menacing gestures, foot-stamping, clap-
ping; and where the victor humiliated the loser, sometimes by
riding around the room on the loser's back. Tsongkhapa, founder of the Gelukpa order in the fourteenth century, characterized
these debates as "contemptuous contradiction": the Merwin-
Trungpa confrontation, seen with Tibetan eyes, is merely tradition.

But Trungpa is not a wise man in the Rockies with a few
students. He has taken the ancient master-disciple relationship
and—having swiftly deciphered the signs of the times—mass-
marketed it. It is at this point that fascism comes into question.
Merwin, in his letter to the Sanders team, writes eloquently on
the topic:

> . . . There was then, in the Vajradhatu, and no doubt there still is,
> a jargon peculiar to the sect, in constant use. It began to flow in at
> once to accommodate what had happened. "Student-teacher rela-
> tionship," "teaching device." "Neurosis" and "aggression," and "ar-
> rogance,"used in special parochial senses. Force directed from on
> top, for instance, is a teaching device, a sort of divine sanction; in-
> fallible. Resistance to it, or any questioning of its aptness is neuro-
> sis, and probably aggressive, because it's a "defense of one's terri-
> tory." Arrogance, despite its dictionary meaning and etymology,
> apparently can apply to anyone *except* the master, whatever he
> does. If everything is to be explained away, or swept behind a veil
> as part of an esoteric "student-teacher relationship," then a great
> deal depends on how much one can trust the teacher, and the
> teacher's attitude to power, as it manifests itself.
>
> Personally, I think that it makes a great difference whether "sur-
> render" and "devotion" to another human being is an individual
> matter, or is made part of the functioning of a group. I think that's
> been one of the repeated teachings of political history. Trungpa—
> then, at least, was surrounded by people who were scared to death
> of him, and he seemed to encourage their feelings of dread, as part
> of their "surrender" and "devotion" to him . . .
>
> Anyway, I wasn't using the word "fascism" loosely. An autocratic
> set-up using organized force, group pressures, fear and informants
> to bring about conformity of attitude and induce "devotion" to an
> individual seems to me to be fascism, even at a classroom level, or

in a street gang. And those who surrender their own judgments, in
a group situation (Naropa and Tilopa, by contrast, were on their
own) to someone they're afraid of, aren't to be trusted, in my opinion.

Buddhist fascism: the fact that Trungpa has even possibly
linked the two words caused Kenneth Rexroth to remark that
"Trungpa has unquestionably done more harm to Buddhism in
the United States than any man living." (He went on, characteristically, to advise immediate deportation: "One Aleister Crowley
was enough for the twentieth century.") The question remains:
Why, of the hundred Buddhist masters now in the U.S., has
Trungpa alone so successfully captured some of the best minds of
the generation?

A possible answer must begin with disgust at America: after
Vietnam, after the failure of the counterculture to produce anything other than some new consumer choices, under the shadow
of the Bomb. Ginsberg:

> And then *I'm* supposed to be like the diplomat poet, defending
> poetry against those horrible alien gooks with their weird Hima-
> layan practices. And American culture! "How dare you criticize
> American culture!" Everybody's been criticizing it for twenty years,
> prophesying the doom of America, how rotten America is. And Bur-
> roughs is talking about "democracy, shit! What we need is a new
> Hitler." Democracy, nothing! They exploded the atomic bomb with-
> out asking us. Everybody's defending American democracy. Ameri-
> can democracy's this thing, this Oothoon. The last civilized refuge
> of the world—after twenty years of denouncing it as the *pits*! You
> know, so now it's the 1970's, everybody wants to go back and say,
> "Oh no, we've got it comfortable. Here are these people invading
> us with their mind control."
> . . . So, yes, it is true that Trungpa is questioning the very foun-
> dations of American democracy. Absolutely! And pointing out that
> the whole—for one thing, he's an atheist. So he's pointing out that
> "In God We Trust" is printed on the money. And that "we were en-
> dowed with certain inalienable rights, including life, liberty and
> the pursuit of happiness." That Merwin has been endowed by his
> *creator* with certain inalienable rights, including life, liberty and
> the pursuit of happiness. Trungpa is asking if there's any deeper ax-
> iomatic basis than some creator coming along and guaranteeing his

rights . . . The whole foundation of American democracy is built
on that, and it's as full of holes as Swiss cheese.

From disgust comes the yearning for apocalyptic change: violence as the only catalyst for the restoration of proper order. The
longed-for revolution of the 1960's never happened. At Naropa,
the dreams of revolutionary romanticism are internalized, trans-
ferred from state to self, a crazy wisdom to face the sane idiocy of
the world. Ginsberg:

> Anything might happen. We might get taken over and eaten by
> Tibetan monsters. All the monsters of the Tibetan Book of the
> Dead might come out and get everybody to take LSD! Actually
> that's what's happening . . . The Pandora's Box of the Bardo
> Thodol has been opened by the arrival in America of one of the
> masters of the secrets of the Tibetan Book of the Dead.

Furthermore, Naropa plays into a central tenet of modernism:
the necessity for aesthetic/spiritual/political elites if the artist is
to survive in the world of mass man. It is no secret that most of
the century's best writers willfully submitted to group authority
(political, spiritual, literary movements), loathed democracy, and
despised at least one other race, religion, class.

Those of us in the "postwar" generation tended to dismiss (or
simply ignore) the politics of our immediate literary ancestors.
We of course—post-war, post-McCarthy, post-segregation, post-
Vietnam—knew better. Ginsberg himself seemed representative
of the "new" poet: emblem of the Bardic tradition, of vision,
song, and resistance to authority. Wherever there was a just
cause—Vietnam, civil rights, nuclear war, and nuclear power—
Ginsberg was highly visible.

In retrospect, however, he seems not a showcase of current
enlightenment, but rather a quirky incarnation in the aristocratic
line. Ginsberg's main activities have never been the championing
of individual rights or the commonweal, but rather the creation
and promotion of elite groups to face the enemy masses: "beats"
vs. "squares"; "heads" vs. "straights"; "peaceniks" vs. "hard-
hats"; and, in a particularly idiosyncratic way, "gays" vs.
"straights" (Ginsberg's poetry is not only anti-"straight," but

also relentlessly misogynistic.) Now Ginsberg's nemesis has become what he calls "the barbarous Western mind," and his need for a ruling elite has found its object in Tibetan theocracy:

> So all of a sudden poets are now confronted by the guys who've got the secrets of the Himalayas! . . . This kind of wisdom was always supposed to be secret. Nobody was supposed to know about it except the gurus and masters of the world, who were ruling everything from the top of the Himalayas . . . And now it's all right here . . .

The masters of the world, ruling everything . . . Pound's vision of the New Order (return to the Old Order) was both more realistic and more Utopic: Mussolini as the possible agent of Confucian "rectification." Ginsberg, however, seems to have driven off the cliff: that *all along* there has been a secret political order to the world, an ancient order to the world that we never knew existed—and now it's ours!

Ginsberg speaks of Naropa and Vajradhatu as an "experiment in monarchy." He believes that Trungpa, like the Pope, is infallible, that the Merwin incident was not a mistake, but a lesson the meaning of which he is not wise enough to decipher. His interview with Tom Clark is, with the Pound radio speeches, the most depressing transcript in American letters.

Naropa, meanwhile, flourishes. Every sensitive kid talks of going there. Such is Ginsberg's power—a refusal to believe in *his* fallibility—that writers and artists who wouldn't be caught dead at, say, a conference sponsored by the Unification Church, gladly sign on for a semester in Boulder. As for Trungpa, let Merwin have the last word: "I wouldn't encourage anyone to become a student of his. I wish him well."

[1980]

Han Yu's Address to the Crocodiles

On the 24th day of the 4th month of the year 819, Han Yu, Governor of Chao-zhou (Canton), instructed his officer Qin Ji to take one sheep and one pig and hurl them into the deep waters of the river Wu as an offering of food for the crocodiles. When the crocodiles had gathered, Han Yu addressed them in the following manner:

"In ancient times, it was the practice of our former Emperors to set the mountains and swamps ablaze, and with nets, ropes, spears, and knives drive beyond the four seas all reptiles, snakes, and malevolent creatures noxious to man. Later, Emperors arose who were of lesser power, unable to maintain an Empire of such vastness. Even the Center was forsaken, let alone here in Chao, between the five peaks and the sea, 10,000 miles from the capital. In that chaos, you crocodiles crept back and multiplied. It was a natural situation under those circumstances.

"Now, however, a true Son of Heaven has ascended the throne: one godlike in wisdom, benevolent in peace, merciless in war. All within the four seas and the six directions is his to rule, administered by governors and prefects whose territories pay tribute to furnish the great sacrifices to Heaven and Earth at the altars of our ancestors and all the gods. These governors and crocodiles cannot share common ground.

"The governor, under the command of the Son of Heaven, has been entrusted with the protection of this land and of its people. But you, bubble-eyed crocodiles, you are not satisfied with the river depths. You take every opportunity to seize and devour people and their livestock, bears and boars, stags and deer, to extend your bellies and multiply your line. You are thus in discord with the governor, and seemingly rival his authority.

"A governor, no matter how feeble, could never bow his head, humble his heart before a crocodile, nor could he stand by in

41

trepidation, shamed before his officers and subjects, acting in an unworthy manner during the existence granted him in this place. Therefore, having received the command of the Son of Heaven to come here as his deputy, he must contend with you, crocodiles. If you have understanding, hear then the governor's words:

"To the south of this province lies the great sea. In it there are places for creatures as great as the whale or shark, insignificant as the shrimp or crab. All there have a home in which to live and eat. If you left this morning, crocodiles, you would be there tonight. Thus I will make this agreement with you:

"Within three days, you must take your hideous brood and head south to the sea, thereby submitting to this appointed deputy of the Son of Heaven. If three days are insufficient, I will allow five. If five days are insufficient, I will allow seven. If, however, after seven days you still linger, with no indication of departure, I will assume that either you have heard and have refused to obey the words of your governor, or else that you are vacant and without reason, incapable of understanding even when a governor speaks to you.

"Those who defy the deputies of the Son of Heaven, who do not listen to their words or refuse to accept them, who from stupidity or lack of intellect harm people and the lesser creatures—such as these will be put to death. The governor will select skilled officers and men who, with strong bows and poison-tipped arrows, shall summarily end this matter, not ceasing, crocodiles, till you all are slain. I therefore recommend that you do not forestall your decision until it is too late."

That night, a violent storm struck the province. When it subsided, some days later, it was discovered that the crocodiles were gone. They were not seen again for a hundred years, when the Empire was again in ruin.

[1980]

Han Yu (768–824): poet, prose master, the leading Tang Confucianist and vehement anti-Buddhist. His "Address" falls at the midpoint of the downward spiral of communication between man and other species from the tribal to the metropolitan.

The Confucian world is a wheel: the Emperor is the hub, his power and authority radiating outward through bureaucratic spokes to encompass everything within the empire. In times of chaos, when the Emperor is weak, when "the center does not hold," everything is possible and in flux. In times of order, each has a fixed place. Thus the crocodiles here are literally trespassers, to be treated like criminals, outlaws from the cosmic contract.

Between the sacred tribal fellowship of hunter and hunted and the metropolitan view of animals as meat-objects or fur-objects or art-objects or obstacles lies this curious Confucian bureaucratic response. Han Yu reads the (not quite apprehended) criminals their rights. They may voluntarily accept the order of the world; if they do not, then divine justice, the word of the Emperor, will be executed. It may well be the last time that men offered the natural world respectfully negotiated terms of surrender.

Paper Tigers

T.

The Maharajah of Rewa, according to his English Adviser, had his own method of hunting tiger:

> He found the easiest way to bag tigers was to take with him a book and a monkey on a long string. When seated in the *machan* [a platform in the trees] he would release the monkey, who immediately climbed into the top branches. He would then give the signal for the beat to start and settle down to read. As soon as the tiger approached the monkey would spot him and give the cough with which all monkeys warn the jungle folk that "Sher Khan" the tiger is on the prowl. His Highness would then quickly put down his book and pick up the rifle.

At the turning of a page, the apparition of a tiger:

Y.

Berggasse 19, March 10, 1933: H. D., one of the last patients of Freud, records her sessions with the Professor:

> Curiously in fantasy I think of a tiger. Myself as a tiger? This tiger may pounce out. Suppose it should attack the frail and delicate old Professor? Do I fear my own terrors of the present situation, the lurking "beast" may or may not destroy him? I mention this tiger as a past nursery fantasy. Suppose it should actually materialize? The Professor says, "I have my protector."
>
> He indicates Yofi, the little lioness curled at his feet.

And a few days later:

> I spoke again of our toy animals and he reminded me of my tiger fantasy. Wasn't there a story, "the woman and the tiger," he asked. I remembered "The Lady or the Tiger."

G.

A King invents a peculiar system of justice: The accused is placed in a large arena before the entire populace and must open one of two identical doors. Behind one, a tiger, which will leap out and tear the man to pieces, establishing his guilt. Behind the other, a lady "most suitable to his years and station," whom he must immediately marry as a reward for his innocence. ("It mattered not that he might already possess a wife and family, or that his affections might be engaged upon an object of his own selection. The King allowed no such subordinate arrangements to interfere with his great scheme of retribution and reward.") The accused, then, must "open either [door] he pleased, without having the slightest idea whether, in the next instant, he was to be devoured or married."

As might be expected, the King has a daughter, and she falls in love with a handsome commoner. Learning of this transgression, the King declares that the boy must be sent to the arena. For one door, the most ferocious tiger in the land is found; for the other, the most beautiful maiden—more beautiful, in fact, than the King's own daughter.

Before the trial, the wily daughter discovers the secret of the doors, and as the boy enters the arena she signals him with her right hand. He immediately opens the right door . . . But which would be worse for this "hot-blooded semi-barbaric princess": to see her beloved ripped to shreds, or happily married to a woman more lovely than she? What was the meaning of her sign? Or, as the story ends: "Which came out of the opened door—the lady, or the tiger?"

E.

Frank Stockton's "The Lady, or the Tiger?," first published in *The Century Magazine* in 1882, quickly became an international obsession. At the time inconclusive endings were vexatious, not modern, and for the twenty years until his death Stockton was besieged with solutions, sequels, and threats. Among the latter, Rudyard Kipling subjected Stockton to a bit of impeccable Raj ragging, as reported by the San Francisco *Wave* in 1896:

Stockton and Kipling met at an author's reception, and after some preliminary talk, the former remarked: "By the way, Kipling, I'm thinking of going over to India some day myself." "Do so, my dear fellow," replied Mr. Kipling, with suspicious warmth of cordiality. "Come as soon as ever you can! And, by the way, do you know what we'll do when we get you out there, away from your friends and family? Well, the first thing will be to lure you out into the jungle and have you seized and bound by our trusty wallahs. Then we'll lay you on your back and have one of our very biggest elephants stand over you and poise his ample forefoot directly over your head. Then I'll say in my most insinuating tones, 'Come now, Stockton, which was it—The Lady or the Tiger?' . . ."

And Mrs. Stockton recorded this ludicrous scene in her diary:

Miss Evans, our niece, wrote to us that a missionary who was visiting her mission station among the Karens [a tribe in northeast Burma], told her she had just come from a distant wild tribe of Karens occasionally visited by missionaries and to her surprise was immediately asked by them if she knew who came out the door, The Lady or the Tiger? Her explanation of it was that some former visitor had read to them this story as suited to their fancy; and as she had just come from the outside world they supposed she could tell the end of it.

Men generally favored the lady, women the tiger. An exception was Robert Browning, who declared he had "no hesitation in supposing that such a princess, under such circumstances, would direct her lover to the tiger's door." In fact, Freud's slip was to the point: it is an *and*, not an *or*, proposition. The choice between lady or tiger, "devoured or married," was to its readers hardly a choice at all. As one W. S. Hopson of San Francisco wrote in 1895:

> When my wife flies into a passion,
> And her anger waxes wroth,
> I think of the Lady and the Tiger,
> And sigh that I chose them both.

R.

A few years after Stockton's death, Elinor Glyn's *Three Weeks* (1907) was the steamy bestseller of its day, its success due largely to its famous seduction scene on a tiger-skin rug:

Paul entered from the terrace. And the loveliest sight of all, in front of the fire, stretched at full length, was his tiger and on him—also at full length—reclined the lady . . .

"No! You mustn't come near me, Paul . . . Not yet. You brought me the tiger. Ah that was good! My beautiful tiger !" And she gave a movement like a snake, of joy to feel its fur under her, while she stretched out her hands and caressed the creature where the hair turned white and black at the side, and was deep and soft.

"Beautiful one! Beautiful one!" she purred. "And I know all your feelings and your passions, and now I have got your skin—for the joy of my skin." And she quivered again with a movement of a snake.

Alas, tiger's fur is short and coarse, and would make for an itchy tryst. But Glyn's book effectively played on the fusion of lady and tiger in the popular imagination. It also inspired this piece of anonymous doggerel (and mnemonic guide to proper pronunciation):

> Would you like to sin
> with Elinor Glyn
> on a tiger skin?
> Or would you prefer
> to err
> with her
> on some other fur?

T.

Tiger, woman, passion. Glin's sin comes out of ancient tradition, for the tiger has always been first female, and later male.

The earliest recorded tigers in the West were those presented to Seleucus I (d. 280 B.C.). (Alexander of course had seen tigers in Persia.) In Latin poetry *tigris* is always feminine (the word means "arrow," and was applied to the swiftness of the animal and the river); in Roman art tigresses are nearly always portrayed. Female tiger is often paired with male lion, much as Freud's "lioness" Yofi checks H. D.'s tiger. Bacchus' chariot was drawn by such a pair. It is a distinction Keats articulates in "Hyperion" as "tiger-passioned, lion-thoughted." (Similarly, the Brontës' cats were named "Tiger" and "Keeper.") As late as the eighteenth century it was believed that the way to capture a tiger cub—the only way to get a tiger for one's menagerie—was the procedure first described by Claudian nearly two thousand years before: steal the cub and, with the tiger in pursuit, scatter mirrors in her path; her female vanity is such that she will gaze fondly in the mirror and forget about the baby.

In China the tiger was originally *yin*: associated with the underworld, and with the West (where the sun enters the underworld). In the *feng-shui* system of geomancy, it is paired with the *yang* green dragon. (The Buddhists would later reverse the genders of the tiger/green dragon pair—stressing the tiger's *yang* nobility, and pointing out, quite correctly, that tigers wear the character for "king," *wang* 王, on their foreheads.) Wordsworth's description (in *The Prelude*) of Jacobin Paris as "Defenceless as a wood where tigers roam" may owe something to Virgil's characterization of Rome as "a wilderness of tigers." But both are identical to the stock Chinese metaphor for a corrupt and sick society: a tiger (*yin*) in a bamboo grove (*yang*), the dark within the light.

Most important is the Chinese tiger-monster, the *tao tie* ("the glutton") which is prominent as early as the Shang dynasty. The *tao tie* is a devourer, and almost always appears in funerary art; sometimes the burial urn itself is in the shape of a tiger. It is the earth eating the dead to provide nourishment for the living—much as the Greek word *sarcophagus* means "to eat flesh." (In the pre-Columbian Americas where there were no tigers, the jaguar was its exact equivalent: an earth-image paired in Mesoamerica with the sky-symbol of the feathered serpent, in South America commonly portrayed in burial urns. The whole city of Cuzco was originally laid out in the form of a jaguar—a kind of living necropolis, *polis* as affirmation of death and life.)

Although frequent in the early Harappan art of the Indus Valley, the tiger is rarely visible as an icon in India until its masculinization in Mughal times—quite strange, considering that Hinduism tended to find metaphysical uses for nearly every indigenous thing. In Hindu iconography it appears only occasionally as the vehicle for the Durga, the terrifying destroyer-goddess. There are, for example, no tigers in Vidyakara's *Treasury*, the great Sanskrit poetry anthology, where so much of Indian life is represented. But among the jungle tribes the tiger was an active presence as devouring mother, fecund mother. "In Akola," writes William Crooke in 1894, "the gardeners are unwilling to inform the sportsmen of the whereabouts of a tiger which may have taken up quarters in their plantation, for they have a superstition that a garden plot loses its fertility from the moment one of these animals is killed." And among the Gonds, wedding ceremonies were marked by the appearance of "two demoniacs possessed by Bagheswar, the tiger god" who "fell ravenously on a bleating kid, and gnawed it with their teeth till it expired."

Y.

Rachel Blau DuPlessis, explicating one of her own poems, writes:

> In "Crowbar," the whole argument comes to the poised end in the doubling of two words: *hungry* and *angry* which grasp towards the odd -*ngry* ending they hold in common. *Hungry* meant complicit with the psychic cultural construction of beautiful, seductive and seduced women; *angry* meant critical of the same.

Hungry woman, angry woman: destroyer, devourer, nurturer: tiger images all. It is curious in this context to read Emily Dickinson's two enigmatic poems on tigers:

566

A Dying Tiger—moaned for Drink—
I hunted all the Sand—
I caught the Dripping of a Rock
And bore it in my Hand—

His Mighty Balls—in death were thick—
But searching—I could see
A Vision on the Retina
Of Water—and of me—

'Twas not my blame—who sped too slow—
'Twas not his blame—who died
While I was reaching him—
But 'twas—the fact that he was dead—

872

As the Starved Maelstrom laps the Navies
As the Vultures teased
Forces the Broods in lonely Valleys
As the Tiger eased

By but a Crumb of Blood, fasts Scarlet
Till he meet a Man
Dainty adorned with Veins and Tissues
And partakes—his Tongue

Cooled by the Morsel for a moment
Growns a fiercer thing
Till he esteem his Dates and Cocoa
A Nutrition mean

I, of a finer Famine
Deem my Supper dry
For but a berry of Domingo
And a Torrid Eye.

G.

There are no tigers in the Bible, and there were no tigers in
medieval Europe—the bestiaries tended to classify them as birds
or snakes. For nearly a thousand years, there were no tigers that
look like tigers in Western art. So, when they began to be im-
ported again into Europe from the animal market of Constanti-
nople at the end of the fifteenth century, they were among the only
creatures with no metaphysical meaning. In the absence of a
fixed iconography, the West had to invent its allegorical tiger.

Shakespeare compares the murderous Queen Margaret (in
Henry VI Part 3) to a tiger, and has Romeo express his rage in
yin imagery:

> The time and my intents are savage-wild,
> More fierce and more inexorable far
> Than empty tigers or the roaring sea.

But he also uses the tiger in its now-familiar masculine role:
symbol of military valor. (Almost all the armies of the world are
decked with tiger images.) Henry the Fifth, in his "Once more
unto the breach, dear friends" speech:

But when the blast of war blows in our ears,
Then imitate the action of the tiger:
Stiffen the sinews, summon up the blood,
Disguise fair nature with hard-favored rage;
Then lend the eye a terrible aspect . . .
Now set the teeth and stretch the nostril wide,
Hold hard the breath and bend up every spirit
To his full height! On, on you noble English . . .

E.

The Western image of the tiger was permanently altered in the eighteenth century by the reign of the Mughal prince Tipu Sultan (1750–99), the self-styled Tiger of Mysore and a perfect incarnation of the perennial Orientalist nightmare of the Eastern despot.

A stern moralist, Tipu abolished polyandry and instituted his version of Koranic law. He changed the calendar and all weights and measures; he renamed all the cities and the towns. He sponsored the arts and commercial enterprises, reformed every detail of daily existence from the way the markets ran to the way crops were planted and gathered. He kept a book of his dreams. At night he slept on the floor on a coarse piece of canvas, and each morning he ate the brains of male sparrows for breakfast.

He commanded an army of 140,000, sworn to wipe out the British. Prisoners were subjected to particularly grotesque torture: boiling oil, special devices for removing noses and upper lips. In his most brilliantly insidious punishment the enemy was turned into the Other: British soldiers were forced to cut off their foreskins and eat them.

He was also, in his mind, a tiger. His throne was mounted on a full-size gilded tiger with rock-crystal eyes and teeth; its finials were tiger heads set with rubies and diamonds; its canopy was tiger-striped with hammered gold. His soldiers dressed in tiger-patterned ("bubberee") jackets and kept their prisoners in tiger cages until it was time for them to be thrown to the tigers. Their cannons had tiger breech-blocks, their mortars were in the shape of crouching tigers, their rifles had tiger-headed stocks and hammers, their swords were engraved with tigers or forged in a striped blend of metals. Live tigers were chained to the palace doors. Tipu's handkerchiefs were striped; his banner read "The Tiger is God."

All this, to put it mildly, made quite an impression in the West. The newspapers were full of Tipu: if an elderly servant was murdered in a siege, she was immediately transformed into four hundred beautiful British virgins throwing themselves on swords rather than face the ravishment of Tipu's troops. In London, Tipu plays were a permanent attraction for thirty years. (The first, *Tippoo Sahib, or British Valour in India,* began running at Covent Garden on June 1, 1791. It was followed the next year by *Tippoo Sultan, or the Siege of Bangalore.*) When Tipu was finally slain and his capital, Seringpatam, captured by the British in 1798, it was cause for national celebration. Robert Ker Porter's 120-foot-long painting, "The Storming of Seringpatam," was mounted on the stage of the Lyceum, and the crowds paid a shilling each to view the great scene. Wilkie Collins in 1868 added an aura to his Moonstone by having it come from the plunder of Seringpatam, and as late as 1898 Sir Henry Newbolt had a popular schlock epic poem on Tipu's defeat.

The tiger, then, took on a fearful androgyny: a masculine military ferocity within a dark Eastern feminine otherness. The tiger was, in the words of Capt. Williamson's *Oriental Field Sports* (1807), "the mottled object of detestation": an obstacle to progress; everything that was not white, Western, male, good. Its literal and metaphorical vanquishing became a British obsession. For a century boys' stories were full of man-eating tigers. With a short leap, the word "man-eater" was soon applied to women.

R.

Blake's "tyger," according to the exegetes, stands for wrath, revolution, untamed energy and beauty, the romantic revolt of imagination against reason. Its direction is East—contrary to the Chinese, but obvious for a Westerner. It is associated with fire and smoke: "burning bright," roaming "in the redounding smoke in forests of affliction," "blinded by the smoke" issuing from "the wild furies" of its own brain. Numerous critics have pointed out that "The Tyger" of *Songs of Experience* was written in 1793, during the French Revolution. But it was also a time when the papers and theaters were crazy with tales of Tipu.

Did Blake ever see a real tiger? The Tower of London menagerie had been opened to the public in the middle of the century (price of admission: three ha'pennies or one dead dog or cat), and it frequently featured tigers. A new specimen was acquired in 1791, the year the first Tipu play opened. And when Blake lived at Fountain Court, the Strand, he could have strolled over to Pidcock's Exhibition of Wild Beasts, where tigers were often on display.

Pidcock and Blake form two sides of a tiger triangle: the third is George Stubbs, the first English painter of tigers. His *The Tyger*, as Kathleen Raine points out in *Blake and the Tradition*, was first exhibited at the Society of Artists of Great Britain in 1769, at the same time and in the same building where the twelve-year-old William Blake was studying drawing at Pars' school. (It was, by the way, Pidcock who sold Stubbs the dead tiger which the artist used for his last work, which bore the matchless title *The Comparative Anatomy of Humans, Chickens & Tigers.*)

Raine remarks on the effect that the painted tiger must have had on the boy Blake. She does not consider, however, the painting itself: Stubbs' "tyger," like all the tigers he painted, is not an icon of untamed energy, but rather a recumbent, noble but cuddly, large cat. (In contrast, his lions are always portrayed committing acts of terror in a storm-tossed landscape—as in the famous *Horse Attacked by a Lion*, now at Yale; a motif Stubbs copied from Roman statuary, which was itself a copy from Scythian art.) And when Blake came to illustrate his "The Tyger" the animal was so oddly passive and sweet, almost smiling, that some friends complained. Shakespeare's hard-favored rage had been disguised by fair nature.

There is no doubt that Blake associated tigers with wrath and revolution, but it is interesting that Blake drew his physical image from Stubbs' painting and the half-dead animals in the local cages—surely he could have imagined it otherwise. (Consider the terror of his flea.) Or is Blake's (and Stubbs') tyger meant to demonstrate the possibilities latent beneath a passive exterior, as yogis traditionally sat immobile on tiger-skin mats, as the men of the industrialized West saw women: a dormant volcano? Is the tyger's blank smile its most fearful symmetry?

T.

It is quite probable that Blake had heard of the death of Sir
Hector Munro's son, the most famous tiger-kills-Englishman
story of the century. This account appeared in *The Gentleman's
Magazine* in July 1793, the year "The Tyger" was composed:

> To describe the aweful, horrid and lamentable accident I have been
> an eye witness of, is impossible. Yesterday morning Mr Downey,
> of the [East India] Company's troops, Lieut. Pyefinch, poor
> Mr Munro and myself went onshore on Saugor Island to shoot
> deer. We saw innumerable tracks of tigers and deer, but still we
> were induced to pursue our sport, and did the whole day. At about
> halfpast three we sat down on the edge of the jungle, to eat some
> cold meat sent us from the ship, and had just commenced our meal,
> when Mr Pyefinch and a black servant told us there was a fine deer
> within six yards of us. Mr Downey and myself immediately jumped
> up to take our guns; mine was the nearest, and I had just laid hold
> of it when I heard a roar, like thunder, and saw an immense tiger
> spring on the unfortunate Munro, who was sitting down. In a mo-
> ment his head was in the beast's mouth, and he rushed into the jun-
> gle with him, with as much ease as I could lift a kitten, tearing
> through the thickest bushes and trees, everything yielding to his
> monstrous strength. The agonies of horror, regret, and, I must say
> fear (for there were two tigers, male and female) rushed on me at
> once. The only effort I could make was to fire at him, though the
> poor youth was still in his mouth. I relied partly on Providence,
> partly on my own aim, and fired a musket. I saw the tiger stagger
> and agitated, and cried out so immediately. Mr Downey then fired
> two shots and I one more. We retired from the jungle, and, a few
> minutes after, Mr Munro came up to us, all over blood, and fell.
> We took him on our backs to the boat, and got every medical assis-
> tance for him from the *Valentine* East India Main, which lay at an-
> chor near the Island, but in vain. He lived twenty four hours in the
> extreme torture; his head and skull were torn and broke to pieces,
> and he was wounded by the claws all over the neck and shoulders;
> but it was better to take him away, though irrecoverable than leave
> him to be devoured limb by limb. We have just read the funeral ser-
> vice over the body, and committed it to the deep. He was an ami-
> able and promising youth. I must observe, there was a large fire
> blazing close to us, composed of ten or a dozen whole trees; I made
> it myself, on purpose to keep the tigers off, as I had always heard it
> would. There were eight or ten of the natives about us; many shots

had been fired at the place, and much noise and laughing at the time; but this ferocious animal disregarded all. The human mind cannot form an idea of the scene; it turned my very soul within me. The beast was about four and a half feet high, and nine long. His head appeared as large as an ox's, his eyes darting fire, and his roar, when he first seized his prey, will never be out of my recollection. We had scarcely pushed our boats from the shore when the tigress made her appearance, raging mad almost, and remained on the sand as long as the distance would allow me to see her.

This scene of the humanly unthinkable, tiger and fire, may have partially inspired Blake. It did most certainly inspire Tipu Sultan. Sir Hector, the boy's father (and ancestor of Hector Hugh Munro, "Saki," whose stories are full of animals attacking people) was the archenemy of Tipu's father, Haidar Ali. At the news of the boy's death—which Tipu gleefully interpreted as a sign that his fellow tigers were joining the struggle against the British—he ordered the construction of a large mechanical toy, now in the Victoria and Albert Museum, to commemorate the event.

It is a lifesize wooden tiger crouched on a prone Englishman. They face each other; the man's left hand touches the tiger's face. They might be mistaken for lovers, but the tiger's teeth are sunk in the man's neck. ("Tipu Sultan," after all, means "Tiger Conqueror of Passion.") Wound up, the toy, simultaneously emits roars and hideous groans. Keats, in "The Cap and Bells," called it the "Man-Tiger-Organ."

Y.

After the fall of Seringpatam, tiger-killing became the standard measure in India of a Britisher's valor and innate superiority. And after the Empire forced peaceful co-existence onto the normally warring princely states, the maharajahs could only display their power and manhood in British terms. No visit to a palace by a distinguished foreigner was complete without a tiger hunt. That the guest would be neither endangered nor disappointed, the tigers were often drugged beforehand with opium-laced meat to ensure a safe and unerring shot.

George Yule of the Bengal Civil Service killed 400 then stopped counting. Colonel Rice killed 93 in four years. Mon-

tague Gerard killed 227. The Maharajah of Surguja killed 1,150.
The Maharajah Scindia killed at least 700. The guests of the
Maharajah Scindia killed at least 200. The Maharajah of Gauri-
piur killed 500 then stopped counting.

As early as 1827, one Capt. Mundy could write, with uninten-
tional irony:

> Thus in the space of about two hours, and within sight of the camp,
> we found and slew three tigers, a piece of good fortune rarely to be
> met with in these modern times, when the spread of cultivation, and
> the zeal of the English sportsmen have almost exterminated the breed
> of these animals.

G.

The Bali tiger: *extinct since 1975.*
The Caspian tiger: 15–20 left, *extinction inevitable.*
The Java tiger: 6–10 left, *extinction inevitable.*
The Sumatra tiger: 700–800 left, *preservation possible.*
The Siberian tiger: 180–200 left, *extinction possible.*
The Chinese tiger: 50–80 left, *extinction probable.*
The Indo-Chinese tiger: 4500–5000 left, *declining rapidly.*
The Bengal tiger: 2500 left, *preservation possible.*

Estimated population of the Bengal tiger, *c.* 1900: 40,000.
Estimated world population of tigers, *c.* 1920: 100,000

Cleansed, the tiger appears in Eliot's "Gerontion" as Christ.

E.

Tigers eat men only when they are starving or are too old or sick to
catch more elusive prey. In parts of India, it is believed that man-
eating tigers are not tigers at all, but men who have transformed
themselves into tigers to commit, for their purposes, masked acts of
murder. These counterfeit tigers, the man-eaters, are recognizable
to the villagers, as they would have been to Freud: they have no
tails.

R.

Jorge Luis Borges, from his half-century of blindness, writes:

> In my childhood I ardently worshiped tigers . . . I used to linger
> endlessly before their cage at the zoo; I judged vast encyclopedias
> and books of natural history by the splendor of their tigers. (I still
> remember those illustrations: I who cannot quite recall the eyes or
> the smile of a woman.)

[1985]

What Were the Questions?

There are only two sources for all of ancient Chinese poetry—two anthologies—and, like nearly everything Chinese, they form a neat pair: *yin* and *yang*, north and south, oral and literary, communal and personal, natural and supernatural, orthodox and heterodox.

The elder of the two is the *Shi jing—The Poetry Classic*, or what Pound called *The Book of Odes*. Reputedly compiled by Confucius himself, it is a collection of 305 songs from northern China, composed between the eighth and sixth centuries B.C. They are anonymous and oral expressions of the workings of the community: planting songs, hunting songs, courtship and marriage songs, hymns, songs to accompany feasts and ceremonies, praises for the rulers. Considered a model artifact of the natural order of human society and the harmony between society and the universe, the *Shi jing* was, for millennia, the primary text of the Confucian canon. Aspiring bureaucrats were required to memorize it for the state examinations. It would, said Confucius, "fire the imagination, perfect one's social graces, straighten out misunderstandings, articulate complaints, instruct in service to one's father, instruct in service to one's lord, and teach the names of birds and beasts, flowers and trees." No literary, philosophical, or political discourse was complete without reference to its authority—usually in the form of a sorely stretched allegorical interpretation.

The shadow side of the *Shi jing* is the *Chu ci—The Words of Chu*, or, as it is known in David Hawkes' classic scholarly translation, *The Songs of the South*. Chu was a small kingdom south of the lands of the earlier Shang and Zhou empires; today it is in central China. It rose in the sixth century B.C. and reached its peak in the fourth, when the earliest poems of the *Chu ci* were written.

A first-century A.D. historian, Ban Gu, has left us this description of the place:

> Watered by the Yangtze and the Han, Chu is a land of lakes and rivers, of well-forested mountains and of the wide lowlands of Jiangnan, where burning and flooding make the labors of plowing and hoeing superfluous. The people live on fish and rice. Hunting, fishing and wood-gathering are their principal activities. Because there is always enough to eat, they are a lazy and improvident folk, laying up no stores for the future, so confident are they that the supply of food and drink will always be replenished. They have no fears of cold or hunger; on the other hand, there are no rich households among them. They believe in the power of shamans and spirits and are much addicted to lewd religious rites.

(trans. Hawkes)

A *triste tropique*: the Chu anthology is a book of shamanistic songs, supernatural journeys, personal confession, nostalgia, enigma, and nearly continual despair.

There are seventeen works—poems and poem-cycles—in the *Chu ci*, half of them written in the fourth and third centuries B.C., and half later imitations. According to tradition, the book was compiled by a librarian named Wang Yi in the second century A.D. Wang himself however—out of modesty or Borgesian humor—claimed that he had merely added a commentary and some (rather dull) poems of his own to the work edited by the librarian Liu Xiang two centuries before. Modern scholars, for their own reasons, don't believe him. Hawkes, for one, believes that the first half—where all the interesting poems are—was collected by Liu An, Prince of Huai-nan, in about 135 B.C., but that Wang Yi was responsible for the second half.

The best-known work in the anthology is the *Li sao* ("On Encountering Sorrow"), a long poem written by Qu Yuan, the first recognizable author in Chinese poetry. It is said that Qu, an honest minister who was banished on trumped-up charges, wrote the poem to protest the injustice of the world, and then drowned himself in the Mi-luo River. [On the day of the Double Fifth festival in South China, people still throw special rice cakes into the rivers to feed his spirit. During the Sino-Japanese war of

1937-45, he was declared the Patriot Poet; after the revolution he became the People's Poet—neither is particularly apt.]

The *Li sao*, one of the great poems in the language—and one that apparently withstands all political weather—begins with the author's birth, continues through a life fraught with injustice and misunderstanding, and then takes off on a shamanistic flight to the other world as the poet searches fruitlessly for a mate among the goddesses and mythical princesses—marriage as allegory for successful employment in the government. In the end, at the peak of heaven, he sees his old home down below, realizes "There are no true men in the state: no one understands me," and decides to kill himself. It is the first in the endless succession of Chinese poems of autobiography, confession, exile, despair. And it is the quintessential *yin* poem: not only rich in flower and water imagery, but also the first poem to incorporate an "empty word" (a meaningless syllable) in the middle of its long lines. Such empty words, in one form or another, became standard practice in much of Chinese poetry: the void around which the poem is constructed, and through which the poem breathes—the void that defines the relationship between things, and between the things and the poet. [Sometimes these empty words are translated as "oh" or "ah," but this is emotional and misleading; most of the time they are simply ignored.]

Also of interest in the anthology is the "Nine Songs" (typical of the book, there are actually eleven). This appears to be a court masque, written for performance with costume, dance, and orchestra, and may also be the work of Qu Yuan. Presumably based on local folk practices, it deals with shamanistic flights and invocations of the gods. Although the texts are now difficult to understand—it is often unclear whether the poet, the shaman, or the god is speaking—the mood is nostalgic, erotic, and relentlessly mournful. The shamans woo the gods and goddesses with tears and lamentation, much like Troubadour lovers. Often the god does not appear; often the meeting is brief. And even those who do achieve ecstatic union with the gods must, too soon, return to the dreariness of the mortal world.

Strangest of all the *Chu ci* texts is the *Tian wen*, a series of 172 questions without answers in 186 lines. Its title has never been explained: *tian* means "heaven," *wen* means "question" (verb or noun). *Tian wen*, then, could be "Heaven's Questions," "Heaven Asks," "Questions About Heaven." Wang Yi thought it meant "Questions to Heaven." Hawkes translates it as "Heavenly Questions," and its most recent translator, Stephen Field, has proposed "Investigation of the Heavens."

The questions begin with the creation of the universe:

> Of the beginning of old,
> Who spoke the tale?
>
> When above and below were not yet formed,
> Who was there to question?
>
> When dark and bright were obscured,
> Who could distinguish?*

move on to astronomy:

> The sun and moon are how coupled?
> How are the patterned stars ranged?

physics:

> Emerge by the boiling canyon.
> Arrive at the vale of night.
>
> From light until dark
> Is a pass of how many miles?

geography:

> How were the Nine Lands blocked?
> How did the rivers clog?
>
> Their eastward flow never fills the sea.
> Who knows why?

marvels of the earth:

---

*The translation cited throughout is by Stephen Field, from his *Tian Wen: A Chinese Book of Origins* (New Directions, 1986). Readers should also consult the more prosaic version by David Hawkes, in his revised version of *The Songs of the South* (Penguin, 1985).

Where is the stone forest?
What beast can speak?

Where roams the Horned Dragon,
Bearing on its back the bear?

mythology:

White serpent in a swirling mist,
Why does it hover about the hall?

From whence came the auspicious pill
That could not well be hidden?

Heaven's Longbow, crosswise in the sky,
When the sun retreated, died.

Why did the Great Bird call,
And thereby lose its life?

and on to legendary heroes and historical kings and princes—
many of them Shang Dynasty figures whose names were unknown from the time the anthology was compiled in the Han
until the recent archeological discoveries—a catalog of conspira-
cies, palace revolts, unjust banishments, adultery, madness, and
murder:

Who would King You have put to death
Had he not received Bao Si?

Heaven's mandate is not assured.
Who is punished, who succored?

Nine times Qi Huan convened the Dukes.
His life was smothered nonetheless.

That stalwart King Chou of Shang,
Who led him into delusion?
. . .

The sages were of equal virtue,
Why were their outcomes so diverse?

Mei Bo was sliced and pickled,
While Ji Zi feigned insanity.

Like all the poems in the *Chu ci*, the questions concerning worldly affairs deal with the decadence and the moral corruption of the times. Amidst the historical, there is this allegorical question:

> Mean creatures are the bees and ants.
> Why is their power pervasive?

Nearly everything about the *Tian wen* is a mystery. Many of the questions are incomprehensible. With the exception of a litany of philosophical questions in the *Zhuangzi*, there is nothing similar in Chinese literature. It was composed in an archaic language, unlike the other poems in the *Chu ci*. It was originally written, like all ancient Chinese books, on slips of bamboo—one line per slip—tied together by string. The string rotted and the lines were shuffled. Its authorship is unknown. Tradition attributes its composition to (again) Qu Yuan, who, seeking refuge in the Chu ancestral temples, wrote the questions as captions for the murals he found on the walls. But this is highly unlikely: there would have had to have been hundreds of murals; and why caption them with questions, or caption them at all? Most vexing to Chinese scholars is the function of the text. What was the "Heavenly Questions" for?

It is obvious what it is not. It is not an examination for students or initiates: some of the answers would be known to the questioner, and some (particularly the cosmological ones) would not. Some of the questions are answered by the following question, and some appear to be riddles or conundrums based on certain information rather than questions about it. It is not a philosophical inquiry, along the lines of the *Zhuangzi* or parts of the *Vedas*: many of the questions are purely historical or scientific, and seem to require short factual answers.

David Hawkes believes it started out as an "ancient, priestly riddle-text (a sort of catechism to be used for mnemonic purposes) which was rewritten and greatly enlarged by a secular poet," whom Hawkes thinks was Qu Yuan. (By "priestly" he means shamanistic, and by "catechism" a truncated one—one without answers.) Stephen Field thinks it was collectively composed by court academicians, "as a debate exercise, created to give the popular and prominent dialecticians a tool for honing their convoluted responses." The great Sinologist Burton Watson has come up with oddest explanation of all, that the questions are in fact "a series of storytellers' topics":

> Thus, for example, if the storyteller began by quoting the passage . . . that reads: "When Chien Ti was in the tower, how did K'u favor her?", his listeners would know that they were about to hear the tale of the ancestress of the Shang dynasty who, shut up in a tower, became pregnant by swallowing a bird's egg sent to her by the hero K'u. Or again, if the storyteller announced: "Lord Millet was the first-born. How did God favor him?", they would settle back to listen to the saga of . . . Lord Millet, the heroic ancestor of the royal family of Chou.

He meets the obvious objection with:

> How the storytellers' "table of topics" came to be compiled in verse form, I do not know, though it seems quite plausible that somewhere along the line an enterprising professional would have delighted in summing up the vast scope of his lore in elegant literary form.

Any of these theories may be correct, or partially correct, but it is also quite possible that the *Tian wen* has no "function" at all—that is, that the questions were composed as, and intended to be, a poem.

Disregarding the later shuffling and possible amendments, I'd like to assume the text has an author, and that the author is Qu Yuan, creator of the *Li sao* and the "Nine Songs." (It could, of course, be a contemporary or later imitator. There used to be a theory that Shakespeare's plays were not written by William Shakespeare, but by another man of the same name.)

Two things about Qu Yuan: First, he is an anti-Confucianist. As the author of the *Li sao*, he has rejected the traditional wisdom that the Mandate of Heaven is bestowed on the good and withdrawn from the evil; his heaven is inscrutable. He has rejected the *Shi jing* notion of the poem as a product of the *vox populi* to write a long poem of his personal sorrow. And he is involved with shamans. Second, he is, as the author of the "Nine Songs," what is now called an ethnopoet: an adapter of archaic religious or indigenous material for a literary audience. (Indeed, the "Nine Songs," with its probable costumes, orchestra, and dances, is reminiscent of the Milhaud-Léger-Cendrars 1923 African spectacle *La Création du monde*.) It is a procedure he would have partially learned from the *Shi jing*, whose songs were regularized and polished to an unknown extent at the time they were collected and written down.

Hawkes has written that "the 'Heavenly Questions' are questions about the parts and motions of Heaven, about the world which it helped produce, and about the various destinies which it dispenses to mortal men." I take this as the poem's argument, the poet's intent. Cheated by heaven, he seeks to understand it by recreating it: a "book of origins," in Field's phrase, or what Pound called "a poem with history." As a book of origins, it is a return—I would say a conscious return—to the origins of lyric poetry: rhythm and taboo.

The poem is written in lines of four characters, each a stressed monosyllable, like most of the poems in the *Shi jing* (which would have been, for Qu Yuan, a primary text of ancient wisdom). This regular, monotonous beat takes us to one of the sources of the lyric: the work song, the lullaby, the dance. Mircea Eliade finds an origin for lyric poetry in the shaman's "preecstatic euphoria"—that is, the chanting and drumming before the shaman takes off to the other world. In all cases, it is assumed that steady physical repetition ultimately flowers into melody and then words.

[Interestingly, the earliest surviving piece of Chinese literary criticism, the "Great Preface" to the *Shi jing*, anonymously written sometime between the fifth century B.C. and the first A.D., has a reverse origin myth for poetry: the words come first. "Poetry is the forward movement of the activities of the mind." (Projective verse!) "When the emotions within one are stimulated into activity, they assume verbal forms. The verbal forms assumed sometimes do not give full expression to the emotions, one has then to have recourse to heaving and sighing. When even heaving and sighing do not give proper vent to the emotions, one turns to chanting and singing. And when even singing and chanting prove unsatisfying, one begins, unwittingly, to gesture and dance with one's entire physical frame." (trans. Siu-kit Wong)]

Perhaps even more important to the evolution of lyric poetry is the fact that the shaman is chanting in a secret language. Metaphor is born from taboo: that which cannot be named must be named in another way. And those who know and can speak the new names have acquired the power of the unnameable. This new magical language invariably takes the form of metrically organized, concentrated speech: the formula. Furthermore, it is nearly always considered to be the language of the lost paradise or of the other world: the language of the gods, the language from the time when men spoke directly with the birds and animals, the language of the kingdom of death.

Arcana is the language of the archaic. It consists of metaphors without referents, weird conjunctions, and meaningless sounds. Once it was spoken in paradise; now, in historical time, it has become incomprehensible to all except a few. It is an image, like the crippled dancer, of the origin: the time when all was one, before things sorted out and the cripple could no longer dance. [In this century, apocalyptically, arcana is the language of the future, the end of time. Joyceans used to say that *Finnegans Wake* would someday be as easy to read as a detective novel; recently, the same claims have been advanced on behalf of the "Language" poets.]

The *Tian wen* is—deliberately, I think—written in the archaic, arcane speech, and overlaid with acronyms, conundrums, and riddles (secular and witty forms of the sacred arcane that—full circle—were often resacralized by religious academics). Whether it is an entirely original composition or an adaptation or "found" poem of shamanistic formulae, with some elaborations, will remain unknown. But what matters is that, as an image of the universe, it was written or compiled or collaged in this way.

Why, then, a poem of questions without answers? The linguist Henry Hiz writes that "the two main views of language, that it describes the world, and that it expresses thought, are not directly applicable to questions." A question is neither true nor false; it is a "suspended thought." The "meaning" of a question, according to Hiz and other linguists, is all its possible answers—or all its true answers.

A question is the only complete grammatical structure that

cannot exist by itself—it must always take us somewhere else, to another sentence or to an unspoken (unspeakable) unknown. It is the piece of ordinary speech closest to a line of poetry. Questions, like poems, like sacred formulae, are articulations of desire. The sacred formula: a concentration of power in order to possess what one does not have, become what one is not. The question: to reach the answer, or the unanswerable. Poetry: to find out, or, in Octavio Paz' phrase, "to find the way out."

Scholars have claimed that Qu Yuan could not be the author of the *Tian wen*, because the poem does not contain the *yin* empty words of the *Li sao*. This is unconvincing: A question contains its own void—it is the pre-eminent *yin* utterance, always unfinished, always "before completion." And nothing could be more anti-Confucian than a question without an answer, for Confucianism, above all, provides answers for everything.

The question, then, may be the perfect vehicle for a poem of origins. It is inherently nostalgic. A question is articulated longing, and there is, finally, only the longing for paradise and its particulars. At the beginning of written poetry, in the earliest surviving texts, there is always the story of the origin, and lamentation for the present decay. In Chinese, the *Li sao* and *Tian wen*. In English, that great poem "The Ruin":

> Snapped rooftrees, towers fallen,
> the work of the Giants, the stonesmiths,
> mouldereth.
> > Rime scoureth gatetowers
> > rime on mortar.
>
> Shattered the showershield, roofs ruined,
> age under-ate them.
> > And the wielders & wrights?
> Earthgrip holds them—gone, long gone,
> fast in gravesgrasp while fifty fathers
> and sons have passed.

A poem that itself ends in ruins:

> Stood stone houses; wide streams welled
> hot from source, and a wall all caught

in its bright bosom, that the baths were
hot at hall's hearth; that was fitting . . .
. . . .
Thence hot streams, loosed, ran over hoar stone
unto the ring-tank. . . .
. . . . It is a kingly thing
. . . . city. . . .

(trans. Michael Alexander)

A question is a quest. A quest that begins with what might
have been the first question ever spoken—and the one most
difficult to answer—"Who's there?" It tracks through the rubble
of the present in search of the origins, the explanations. In the *Li
sao*, Qu Yuan goes to heaven to understand earth; in the *Tian
wen* he wanders with seeming aimlessness through human history to understand heaven.

China has never had an epic poem; the *Tian wen* is its first,
and best, "poem with history." And *historiai*, what Herodotus
called his book about the Persian Wars, means "a learning or
knowing by inquiry." The Greek verb *historein* means "to ask
questions."

History, in the *Tian wen*, is an endless reiteration of moral
corruption and legal crime. It is possible to imagine Qu Yuan as
Job: that his questions are rhetorical, not meant to seek answers,
but only to bewail the injustice of heaven. I'd prefer to think of
him as Perceval or one of the heroes of countless fairy tales: those
who discover that asking the question is not only an act of
personal redemption, but a way to save the state.

[1986]

Postscript

There is a *yin* and *yang* of poetry: poems that ask questions
and those that claim to have the answers. Thinking about the
Tian wen, I find it hardly a coincidence that the two great writers
of questions in twentieth-century American poetry were both
women: H. D., particularly in her late poetry of nostalgia, elegy,
and recalled passion:

He went away, Goth, the German, *Germain*,
degrees, days, hours, minutes,

how many? he left the flowers, August the 3rd,
this is October 17th and they say,

he comes back in three days—will he?
who will come back? a wandering flame,

a name, Goth, Gott, *Dieu admirable*, or another?
what Sun will rise, what darkness will unclose?

what spark, diastole, systole, compel, repel?
what counter-appeal contract the heart?

or not, what mystery? shall the winter-branch
be broken, fuel for another? or shall the branch,

prouder than spring, lordlier than summer,
strike deeper and grow higher to disclose

the last enchantment,
the white winter-rose?

And Gertrude Stein, dynamiter of syntactical authority—whose last words were, reputedly, "What is the question?":

Why is a pale white not paler than blue, why is a connection made by a stove, why is the example which is mentioned not shown to be the same, why is there no adjustment between the place and the separate attention. Why is there a choice in gamboling. Why is there no necessary dull stable, why is there a single piece of any color, why is there that sensible silence. Why is there the resistance in a mixture, why is there no poster, why is there that in the window, why is there no suggester, why is there no window, why is there no oyster closer. Why is there a circular diminisher, why is there a bather, why is there no scraper, why is there a dinner, why is there a bell-ringer, why is there a duster, why is there a section of a similar resemblance, why is there that scissor.

South, south which is a wind is not rain, does silence choke speech or does it not.

A Few Don'ts for Chinese Poets

The split between the *Shi jing* and the *Chu ci,* between a poetry of the community and a poetry of the individual, has remained a topic of debate in Chinese poetry for millennia. At the birth of the People's Republic in 1949, Mao Zedong in his famous Yan'an Talks, declared that poetry should be based on folk songs and classical Chinese prosody, and concern itself solely with the ramifications of the class struggle. Discussion was effectively closed for thirty years. But since Mao's death in 1976 and the subsequent fall of the Gang of Four, the controversy has heated up again, this time over the appearance of a new kind of writing that has been called Obscure Poetry.

Obscure Poetry is being written by poets in their twenties and thirties: its best-known practitioners include two men, Bei Dao (b. 1950) and Gu Cheng (b. 1957), and a woman, Shu Ting (b. 1952). They belong to the Mao generation: those born shortly after the Revolution, and who reached adolescence in the Cultural Revolution (1966–76). Urban children of professional workers and intellectuals, they were encouraged to join one of the factions of the Red Brigades to revivify the Revolution and purify the country. Each faction, in turn, was humiliated and defeated. With all schools closed and intellectual pursuits forbidden, they were sent to the provinces to work in the farm brigades. There they were appalled by the poverty of peasant life, the apparent failure of the Revolution to effect much change in the vastness of the country. After the death of Mao, the schools reopened with a clamorous drive toward technology and modernization. But the youth brigade was no longer young. There was no room for them in the classrooms—a new generation had to be trained. They remained uneducated, disillusioned, and (many of them) unemployed. For mentors they discovered the surviving intellectuals newly released from the Cultural Revolution's prisons and exile.

In the late 1970's, their work began appearing in underground magazines, on wall posters, and at mass poetry readings in the parks (the first since the Revolution). It rejected "class struggle" and "promotion of productivity" as the only suitable themes for poetry, and emphasized expressions of the self: love, pain, introspection, solitude. It further declared its freedom from the "stubborn grip of artistic convention," the classical prosodies and folk songs; the new poetry was all written in free verse. Their manifestoes and statements sounded like this:

> Yang Lian: Having poetry serve as political propaganda is a misfortune that should have stopped long ago! Too long has poetry remained enslaved, subject to the juggling acts of political careerists furthering their own ambitions. If some today still require that poetry bear a "political label," they are either muddleheaded or malicious!

> Ling Bing: I'm opposed to "tradition," and I'm opposed to stereotyped style and its stranglehold on people's souls.

> Bei Dao: Poetry has no boundaries, not those of time, space, or the self. But the starting point of poetry should be the poet's self.

> Shu Ting: I'm ready to use poetry to express my concern for the human race to the fullest. Obstacles must be removed, masks should be torn off.

> > (Trans. Pan Yuan & Pan Jie)

To the charge that they were writing "obscure" poetry, they replied, not surprisingly, "If you cannot understand, your son or grandson will understand some day."

The establishment, poets and critics of the social realism generations, came down heavily on them. The new poetry was "disgraceful," "denigrative," "walking a dangerous path," "a trend that ruins the name of vernacular poetry, poisons some people, and is deeply resented by many readers," "a betrayal of tradition." The poet Ruan Zhangying wrote that "works that advocate personal feelings . . . are not accountable to society . . . they create spiritual pollution." And the critic Cheng Daixi claimed that expression of the self was merely "bourgeois or petit-bourgeois individualism and anti-rational anarchism," and that "ob-

scurity, absurdity, vagueness, and difficulty" reflect only the
"hopelessness, emptiness, and desperation" of Western capitalism. Almost inevitably in the myth-making processes of Marxist
countries, the anti-Obscurists even managed to produce a Tai-
wanese writer of free verse who had recanted: "I am against
modernism, for I see the smallness of the self and the greatness of
history."

[As an example of the kind of poetry the establishment still
promotes, the Sinologist William Tay cites this excerpt from a
200-line rhymed narrative poem on the ups and downs of the
recently rehabilitated Marshall Peng Dehui—a prize-winning
work chosen from hundreds of thousands in 1980, just at the
moment when Obscure Poetry was making its greatest splash:

> Three years are not very long,
> The present and the past, what a change.
> Truth always lies with the Communists,
> I certainly won't drown myself like Qu Yuan!
>
> The roads are long, but I'll keep searching,
> My search for truth is for the Party.
> Punished and dismissed, I am not daunted,
> For the truth will reach the Party Central Committee.

How strange to find Qu Yuan in a context that would have made
him queasy. In the end, the outcasts make the most enduring
monuments: the U.S. has shopping centers and elementary
schools named after Walt Whitman; Peru has declared César
Vallejo its national poet; France has put an enormous portrait of
Rimbaud on a public housing development—can Artaud General Hospital be far behind?]

So what, finally, is Obscure Poetry? It turns out to be, of all
things, pure Imagism:

> *Feeling*
> The sky is grey
> The road is grey
> The building is grey
> The rain is grey

In this blanket dead grey
Two children walk by
One bright red
One pale green

                                      (Gu Cheng)

Life
Net

    (Bei Dao)

Wrinkles
Ruts left on my body
By the reversed wheels of history.

                                      (Cai Kun)

                        (trans. William Tay)

What is remarkable is that these poets seem to have invented
Imagism on their own. Having received no education, and having had very little material available to them for self-education,
they were, by all accounts, entirely unaware of Western early
modernism at the time these poems were written. Nor did they
know that Imagism had been invented (or reinvented) in China
seventy years before.

It was one of the neater symmetries of modernism: the East
discovering in the West what the West had found in the East.
Ezra Pound, in 1913, shortly after receiving the Fenollosa manuscripts of Chinese poetry, writes "A Few Don'ts by an Imagiste,"
surely the most influential manifesto in English in this century.
Published in *Poetry* that year, it is enthusiastically read by a
young Chinese poet named Hu Shi, who is studying in the
United States. Hu returns to China and, in 1917, publishes his
"Tentative Proposals for the Improvement of Literature" which
quickly becomes known as the "Eight Don'ts." ("Write with
substance . . . Don't imitate the ancients . . . Emphasize gram-
mar . . . Reject melancholy . . . Eliminate old clichés . . . Don't

use allusions . . . Don't use couplets and parallelisms . . . Don't avoid popular expressions or popular forms . . .") The following year Hu Shi waves the banner of the new in a series of even more Poundian formulations ("Speak only if you have something to say . . . Say what you have to say, and say it as it is said . . . Speak your own language, not the language of others . . . Speak the language of your own time.") These manifestoes set off a literary revolution, the May Fourth Movement of 1919, which runs parallel to the political fervors of the moment: nationalism and progressiveness, the rejection of traditional models, a denunciation of Western political dominance combined (unironically) with enthusiasm for all things Western, and a rallying to replace *wen yan* (classical literary writing) with *bai hua* (popular speech).

Hu Shi, in turn, seemed to be unaware that many of the precepts of Imagism had been formulated—in China of course—centuries before by the poet-critic Yuan Haowen (1190–1257).

Yuan was a poet-critic in the true sense: that is, most of his criticism was written in verse form—a genre which seems to have dropped out of world literature. He wrote during the obscure and short-lived Jin Dynasty, which he saw fall to the Mongol invaders, whom he refused to serve. He is best known for a series of 30 "Poems on Poetry," some scattered poems on the fall of the dynasty, prefaces to collections by Du Fu and Su Dongpo, and his anthology of Jin poetry, the function of which he described in a moving poem:

> In times of peace, there's no need for unofficial recorders;
> But since the disaster, everything has been destroyed, even the
>   official histories.
> Thanks to heaven, a manuscript of the century's work has been
>   preserved;
> I take it to the lonely hills to read with stifled tears.*

Yuan's critical admonitions—in favor of "sincerity" and colloquial speech, against ornamentation and slavish imitation of the ancients—had no immediate impact. He wrote, after all, during one of the collapses of the Empire, and—refreshingly, for a

---

*The translations of Yuan are adapted from John Timothy Wixted's monograph *Poems on Poetry: Literary Criticism of Yuan Hao-wen*; Wiesbaden: Franz Steiner Verlag, 1982.

critic—his most important critical work, the "Poems on Poetry,"
were written for his own illumination, and were not circulated.
But he was never obscure, and earlier in this century the great
scholar Kojiro Yoshikawa even declared that Yuan was a greater
poet than his Song Dynasty near-contemporaries, Lu Yu and Su
Dongpo. This is hard to believe, but much of what Yuan wrote is
still worth reading:

> Write verse the way you speak! What need to display one's talent?

> . . . fashionable adornment,
> Rouge and tint, struggle uselessly to gain affection.

> You can rarely know a man from his writings.

> Naturally inspired is the line where the eye gives shape to the
> mind.

> Without sincerity there is nothing. Unless one is sincere, there is
> nothing by which to guide one's words, and the heart and the
> mouth separate into two objects. One becomes estranged from the
> world and one's words grow apart from things, becoming vaguer
> with distance. Coming from afar, one's words, though they be
> heard, will be like spring breezes blowing past the ears of a horse.

> . . . to get away from the ordinary and the hackneyed, to wash clean
> hazy obscurities, to range freely over the realm of one's potential as
> if smashing an enemy formation or capturing monsters, to expli-
> cate what is hidden, to encompass past and present, to vie with crea-
> tion itself—this is skill. Dull-witted obscurity, superficial rashness,
> indulgent license, trumped-up trivialities, rotten clichés—these are
> faults.

> Tang Geng said: When poetic discipline suffers from strictness, it
> approaches meanness.

> What does a poet know of the mechanism that makes all things
> work?
> To find and use a single key is more than enough.

And Yuan himself wrote a "Few Don'ts" for Chinese poets.
Allowing for some cultural translation, they are still apt:

Don't be unhappy.
Don't be slick.
Don't be fiercely sharp.
Don't be pointedly disagreeable.
Don't be deviously incriminating.
Don't be wishy-washy.
Don't draw far-fetched conclusions.
Don't curry favor.
Don't practice self-advertisement.
Don't wear camouflage.
Don't indulge in sophistries.
Don't act as if you're some great sage.
Don't be as jealous as a concubine.
Don't be a malicious feuder.
Don't be a rabble-rousing rumor-monger.
Don't be a blind face-reader.
Don't be a drunk abusive condemned criminal.
Don't be a wise guy doing "favors" that cost nothing.
Don't be a stubborn old farmer.
Don't be a mercilessly unrelenting prosecutor.
Dont be one who sells another's goods.
Don't be a singer in the market whining about ill treatment.
Don't be a *pipa* player rhyming phrases about the soul.
Don't be a village schoolmaster with a how-to-write book.
Don't be a sand-counting monk getting lost in semantics.
Don't be an exorcist slinging taboo words.
Don't act as if you're the only person in the universe or the
    only one in the history of time.
Don't get unruffled by petty offenses.
Say nothing that isn't true.

At the end of his life, immersed in Chan Buddhism, he wrote a series of four poems titled "On Being Called to Write." Here is one of them:

> In a dream, startled that my hair had turned white,
> I wrote a poem as I would speak it, and yet it was divine.
> In heaven, the price of poetry has gone up:
> For even one good stanza, one has to pay with one's youth.

That last line could be a fit epitaph for the Obscure Poets of the Mao generation. I wonder, but doubt that they know it.

[1986]

Kampuchea

1

In 1969, there were 7,000,000 people in Cambodia. 90% of the peasants owned their own land, and the country, producing more food than it needed, shipped rice abroad. The government, such as it was, was ruled by Prince Norodom Sihanouk, who was popular among the peasantry and despised by the middle class. Despite personal excesses, he had successfully maintained Cambodia's neutrality through the Southeast Asian wars. Leftist guerrillas, whom Sihanouk called "Khmer Rouge," had a few hundred troops in the mountains.

On March 18, 1969, the aerial bombardment of Cambodia by the United States began. These were the secret "Menu" operations—Breakfast, Lunch, Supper, Dinner, Dessert, Snack—and their purpose was the destruction of Viet Cong and North Vietnamese supply lines and "sanctuaries." They were a military failure, and an unknown number of Cambodian civilians were killed.

On March 18, 1970, the government of Sihanouk was overthrown by Lon Nol, the Prime Minister whose personality, mirrored back on itself, was said to be as palindromic as his name. His press conferences alternated between long silences and lectures on ancient Khmer history. Within a year he was a stroke victim. Yet he remained in power, his presence giving U.S. and Cambodian officers and bureaucrats free reign.

Six weeks after the March coup, American and the particularly cruel South Vietnamese troops entered Cambodia. The bombardment became public and regular. From 1969 to 1973, the United States dropped 1,078,258,000 pounds of bombs on the country. The larger bombs created craters 18 feet deep and 60 feet in diameter.

By 1974, 80% of the rice paddies were abandoned, 75% of the draft animals destroyed. Millions were refugees, fleeing the American planes, the South Vietnamese troops, and the Khmer Rouge who, as the only opposition to Lon Nol, had grown numerous and strong. The economy shifted from agriculture to one based on arms and the jetsam of troops. Fortunes were made by officials and merchants. For the rest, starvation was prevalent. A bowl of soup which had cost 4 riels in 1970, now cost 300. In the capital, Phnom Penh, now five times its prewar population, most of the trees had died, their bark stripped and eaten. Animals in the zoo were eaten.

By 1975, 500,000 Cambodians were dead.

On April 17, 1975, the Khmer Rouge entered Phnom Penh. Cambodia was renamed Democratic Kampuchea, and the 2,000,000 inhabitants of the city, as well as those in the other cities and large towns, were immediately forced to evacuate, regardless of age or health.

The people were divided into three categories. The first group, known as the "Old People," were Khmer Rouge supporters and those who lived in previously liberated areas of the country. The second group, the "New People," were those from the unliberated pockets, mainly the cities. The third group included those who had worked in the Lon Nol regime as civil servants, police, soldiers. Beyond this taxonomy were the larger minorities: Chinese, Vietnamese, and the Cham, an Islamic people.

The third group and their families were quickly executed. The minorities were exiled or killed. The "New People" were marched into the countryside where, under the direction of "Old People," everyone over the age of six worked in the paddies or on huge irrigation projects in brigades as large as 20,000. They worked 18 hours a day for no wages. The pieces of canals they built did not link; their dams could not hold water. While many of the workers died of starvation, what rice they harvested was packed and shipped to an unknown destination.

Each "new" person was required to prepare an autobiography. On the basis of these texts, enemies of the state were discovered and eliminated: doctors, technicians, Buddhist monks, teachers, intellectuals, students. Anyone who had studied abroad was killed, anyone who spoke French, anyone with fair skin, anyone who wore glasses. Survival was possible only for those who successfully obscured their pasts.

Overseas Cambodians were urged to return to their country to build Kampuchea. About a 1000 did so, and 85 survived. It is also said that:

—Of 50,000 monks, 900 survived;
—Of 300 journalists, 5 survived;
—Of 416 art students, 14 survived;
—Of 41 librarians, 6 survived;
—Of 24,336 teachers and professors, 3050 survived.

The slogan for the "New People" was:

> PRESERVE THEM—NO PROFIT!
> EXTERMINATE THEM—NO LOSS!
> WE WILL BURN THE OLD GRASS
> AND THE NEW WILL GROW.

To save ammunition, victims were clubbed to death, or had their throats slit with a notched sliver of bamboo. Babies were tossed into the air to be caught on the point of a bayonet. The craters left by the American bombs were used for mass graves.

All books, wristwatches, radios, cameras, television sets, individual cooking utensils, musical instruments, religious objects, family photographs, and works of art were destroyed. All Buddhist shrines and pagodas, all schools, universities, libraries, and theaters were razed or turned into storehouses, pigsties, prisons. In Phnom Penh the Catholic Church was dismantled stone by stone. Street signs in the deserted city were painted over, white.

Kampuchean women and girls were required to wear their hair short. All citizens dressed in black; one suit of clothes per year was issued. Existing families were broken up; marriages required state approval and were held once a year in mass ceremony. Living quarters—large dormitories with long sleeping platforms—were segregated by sex and age. Non-conjugal sex was prohibited, as were all holidays, festivals, public and private pleasure activities.

There was no currency, no Western medicine, no postal service, no telegraph, no telephones. No conversation was allowed after dark, and no foreign words could be spoken. A four-page newspaper was published rarely, and was not available to the public. Radio Phnom Penh was played over loudspeakers in the fields. This was the national anthem, in the official translation:

> Bright red Blood which covers towns and plains
> Of Kampuchea, our motherland,
> Sublime Blood of workers and peasants,
> Sublime Blood of revolutionary men and women fighters!
>
> The Blood changing into unrelenting hatred
> And resolute struggle,
> On April 17th, under the flag of Revolution,
> Free from slavery!

There were no schools for children over ten. (Khieu Samphan, a founder of the Khmer Rouge, had said, "The more man is educated, the more deceitful he becomes.") Those younger attended one hour or less a day, memorizing songs and slogans. Reading and writing were prohibited throughout the country. Children who misbehaved in class were killed in front of their classmates. Sometimes the children were required to kill their classmates. Young soldiers received daily training in the "cruelty game": clubbing dogs and cats, setting cages of mice on fire, chopping off the tails of monkeys, feeding the monkeys—or occasionally children—alive to the crocodiles.

Kampucheans were instructed to emulate not the ant or bee, but the ox: it works when it is told to work, eats where it is told to eat, lives always under yoke or tether. They were to live in the spirit of three renunciations: renunciation of personal attitudes, renunciation of material goods, renunciation of personal behavior. (Khieu Samphan had said: "We will be the first nation to create a completely Communist society without wasting time on intermediate steps.")

No leaders were mentioned by name. Kampucheans were told only to obey *Angka*, the Organization, and its local representatives, the peasant district leaders and the young boys with submachine guns. The country was completely sealed from the outside world; in the West Khieu Samphan was believed to be the head of *Angka*.

On September 29, 1977, more than two years after the Khmer Rouge victory, Pol Pot appeared in Peking to announce that *Angka* was in fact the Communist Party, and that he was both head of the Party and Prime Minister of Kampuchea. Following purges and shifts of power still unknown, a ruling quaternity had emerged: Pol Pot, Ieng Sary, and their wives, Khieu Ponnary and Khieu Thirith, who were sisters. Khieu Samphan was revealed to be merely a figurehead.

Little is known of Pol Pot. He has rarely spoken in public, been interviewed or photographed. His few public statements sound like this: "More and more friends do come to visit Kampuchea, but we have to make our country neater and more beautiful before we can receive guests." Or: "In terms of material achievement, such as factories, grain output, cultural activities and so on, performances have been modest, but we are very pleased with the development of the revolutionary movement of the masses."

He was born in 1928, and spent six years, like many Cambodian men, as a Buddhist monk. He went to Paris in 1949 to study radio electronics; returned to Phnom Penh in the early 1950's to teach at a private school; became a well-known journalist; and was Deputy Secretary General of the underground Communist Party in 1962. In 1963 he disappeared for a dozen years. His name is a pseudonym.

Pol Pot's vision of Kampuchea was modeled on the reign of Suryavaram II, the twelfth-century ruler whose slaves built Angkor Wat and an elaborate hydraulic system. In Khmer, the word for "revolution" is *bâmbah-bàmbor* ("uprising" plus "reconstruction"). Under Pol Pot, the word used for "revolution" was *pativattana* ("return to the past").

On January 7, 1979, the Vietnamese army captured Phnom Penh, ending the Pol Pot regime. In the three years and nine months of Democratic Kampuchea, some 2,000,000 had died of execution, starvation, exhaustion.

The retreating Khmer Rouge troops burned fields and granaries. In the chaos of displaced millions attempting to return to their villages or find surviving family members, there was little production of food. It is said that 700,000 died in the resulting famine.

2

The "slaughter" by the Khmer Rouge, said Noam Chomsky in 1977, *is a New York Times invention.*

As an ideologue, he was wrong. But as a linguist? What is *slaughter*? An accident of speech, easily mistyped into *laughter.* A word without reference for most of us, a word to be placed in quotation marks, taken on hearsay—an invention. And what is Kampuchea for us, the outsiders, but the inventions of *The New York Times*—and the stacks of United Nations reports, the microfilmed documents that whirred past my eyes in a library basement, the tales of ideologically selected survivors, the autopsies and revisions performed by journalists, "experts," and the politically convinced.

Kampuchea is nothing for us but a heap of words, and a few photographs: the piles of skulls; the map of the country, now on exhibit, made of human bones and hair; the sign of the security regulations in Tuol Seng prison, now translated for visitors:

1. YOU MUST ANSWER ACCORDINGLY TO MY QUESTIONS. DON'T TURN THEM AWAY.
2. DON'T TRY TO HIDE THE FACTS BY MAKING PRETEXTS THIS AND THAT. YOU ARE STRICTLY PROHIBITED TO CONTEST ME.
3. DON'T BE A FOOL FOR YOU ARE A CHAP WHO DARE TO THWART THE REVOLUTION.
4. YOU MUST IMMEDIATELY ANSWER MY QUESTIONS WITHOUT WASTING TIME TO REFLECT.
5. DON'T TELL ME EITHER ABOUT YOUR IMMORALITIES OR THE ESSENCE OF THE REVOLUTION.
6. WHILE GETTING LASHES OR ELECTRIFICATION YOU MUST NOT CRY AT ALL.
7. DO NOTHING. SIT STILL AND WAIT FOR MY ORDERS. IF THERE IS NO ORDER, KEEP QUIET. WHEN I ASK YOU TO DO SOMETHING, YOU MUST DO IT RIGHT AWAY WITHOUT PROTESTING.
8. DON'T MAKE PRETEXTS ABOUT KAMPUCHEA KROM IN ORDER TO HIDE YOUR JAW OF TRAITOR.

9. IF YOU DON'T FOLLOW ALL THE ABOVE RULES, YOU WILL GET MANY MANY LASHES OF ELECTRIC WIRE.

10. IF YOU DISOBEY ANY POINT OF MY REGULATIONS YOU WILL GET EITHER TEN LASHES OR FIVE SHOCKS OF ELECTRICAL DISCHARGE.

and the rare portrait of Pol Pot, transmitted by satellite from Peking in 1977: a middle-aged man with a pear-shaped head, a crewcut, eyes that stare into the camera, mouth a printed smudge—a face one wouldn't recognize on the street, the face of a police composite.

It is a heap of words, facts, and specimens of local speech to be arranged on the page as I have done. Trying to think about Kampuchea, I begin in the only way I know how, by laying out the details: a little anthology, a still life (or more exactly, grim joke, a *nature morte*). I add it up, and try to find the word that equals the sum, hoping that a word is the beginning of understanding. Not *genocide*, a legal term for a specific kind of mass murder, and not applicable here where killer and killed are indistinguishable. Not *holocaust*, that certain fire in history, a word that belongs to its moment. Not *atrocity, horror, disaster*, for they are now the stuff of everyday speech, their referents ranging from Hiroshima to Hollywood. There is, I think, only one word for what occurred in Cambodia during those three years and nine months: *Kampuchea*. A word with no other meaning, a word that doubles back on itself.

Kampuchea is a word with no synonym, for Kampuchea was, above all, a totality, an entity complete unto itself. And more—it was a work of art, a fully realized act of the imagination, a vision fulfilled, Utopia. It was all of these things—if we take the words *art, imagination, vision, Utopia* to mean their opposites, to stand for words we do not possess: an art, an imagination, a vision, a Utopia in the service of destruction, in the service of death.

Kampuchea was, according to Ieng Sary, "something that never was before in history." Other bloodthirsty nations have had their logic, however barbaric. In ideological societies, a certain kind of human, or human behavior, is perceived as the *enemy*, the obstacle that must be eliminated (through war, genocide, purge) if that society is to be perfected. In some religious societies, an artificial cycle of life and death (sacrifice and rebirth) must be maintained to ensure the continuance of the cosmic cycle. In the recent cults of mass suicide, there is the belief that we are only here on earth as a way station to the paradise beyond death. But in Kampuchea, man himself was the enemy—the works of man, human acts, human nature.

Like all Utopias, it was dedicated to the creation of a New Man—but a New Man so unrecognizable that to think about Kampuchea, to try to think about Kampuchea, is to find oneself in an imagination that cannot be imagined; a world where, as in the streets of Phnom Penh, the signs are painted over, white. There everything is the same, but different. A sign is a sign, but it is illegible, even to the inhabitants. And yet it is still a sign . . .

Each image of Kampuchea begins in familiarity and ends in another world. I think of misbehaving as a boy in school, and then I imagine being killed there on the spot for it. I think of that universal gesture of throwing a small child in the air: the screams of the child, half-fear, half-delight; the hands of the adult or elder child reaching up. It is at the edge of the social contract: power used for the production of pleasure, the domestic benevolent dictatorship. Every mind has this memory—as child, as adult, as observer. But to imagine Kampuchea is to see (or to be) that child falling through the air, falling not toward the familiar out-stretched hands, but onto the point of a bayonet.

The perversion of the routine gesture is a commonplace of political history: the prince is handed the goblet of wine, and the wine is poisoned. (Today one starts one's car and the car blows up, one opens a letter and the letter blows up. A microcosm of the nuclear disaster: when the Bomb goes off, we will all be inciner-ated in the middle of the most ordinary tasks.) But what is particularly Kampuchean was the elaborate variety, the multipli-cations of this perversion of the everyday. In Kampuchea, almost any gesture led to death.

It is easy to imagine oneself as a victim. (I wear glasses; I know foreign languages; I write . . .) But such thinking becomes a literal dead end: to imagine oneself as dead is not to think about Kampuchea at all. Nor is it difficult, raised on images of murder, to imagine oneself, at least once, as a murderer. But Kampuchea was something more. It requires that one imagine oneself as a murderer in a society where all the living are murderers or accomplices, where there are no demarcated groups of murderers and murdered, where murder is the ordinary, and eating, sleeping, making love, making conversation, making art, the extraordinary. To think about Kampuchea one must imagine, not acts of murder, nor death itself, but a life of death. And it is here where my mind blanks out. Absolute horror, like bliss, is a world from which human speech cannot return.

I find myself circling back around the figure of Pol Pot, trying to read that almost blank page. He has at least one historical predecessor, the Chinese general Zhang Xian-zhong, who slaughtered the 100,000 inhabitants of a Sichuan city in the seventeenth century, and then erected a stone to commemorate the event, with this inscription:

HEAVEN BESTOWS A HUNDRED GRAINS UPON MANKIND.
MAN OFFERS NOT A SINGLE GOOD DEED TO RECOM-
  PENSE HEAVEN.
KILL. KILL. KILL. KILL. KILL. KILL. KILL.

[Zhang Xian-zhong believed that he himself was not a man, but the incarnation of a star sent down by the Jade Emperor to kill all men. And though he particularly relished the death of scholars, he also thought of himself, through a coincidence of names, as the god of literature.] Yet what is most remarkable about Pol Pot is that, perhaps uniquely in history, he was a despot who erected no stones to himself, no "personality cults," no icons. He was the invisible ruler: both the throne and the power behind the throne.

In the absence of concrete information, I cast about for clues, and I land on his years in radio electronics. The radio leads me, like most roads, to poetry. Since its invention, radio has become a frequent metaphor for the poetic process: the poet as vehicle of the muse has become the poet as antenna of the race. The words are out there; writing is a kind of "tuning in."

In this context, Ezra Pound's World War II broadcasts become a full-scale classical tragedy. Not the beliefs expressed and his Fascist partisanship; that is merely loathsome. What is tragic was this act of *hubris*: the poet attempting to become the muse.

Pol Pot too, remaining invisible, wanted to be (and became, as Pound never did) that bodiless Voice. It is the Voice that tells us to go on the mountain and slay our son; the Voice that tells us, suddenly, to kill a dozen people in a restaurant; the Voice that tells the thousands to erect the pyramids of sacrifice and the extermination camps; the Voice that sends us into battle. (How different is it, I wonder, from the Voice that dictates the next line?) And more, he was the Voice that spoke to the voices that spoke: in Kampuchea all forms of communication were outlawed, except the radio. Yet Pol Pot himself was rarely, perhaps never heard.

To be not only poet, but muse; to become inspiration itself. To be not only king, but kingship: to dissolve into pure power. It has been the dream of centuries: to become the invisible worm, the force that blocks reason and impels some poor peasant to run a bayonet through a child. Can such a story ever be known? What words could tell it?

[1982]

II

EXTENSIONS
OF POETRY

A Little Heap for George Oppen

The boy lived, in New Rochelle, on one Wildcliff Road: a short street of large houses leading to Long Island Sound. Words then, from the beginning, meant more or meant less than they said: Wildcliff Road has no cliffs and is not wild; and "sound" is the first pun every local kid learns: music and water.

A neighbor, for a few of those years, was D. W. Griffith, whose studio was nearby in Mamaroneck. They may never have met, though the child later mastered and adapted certain of the director's inventions. The *close-up* and the *iris*: the isolation of the particular in the panorama of history or of culture. *Parallel cutting*: the story or poem projected forward through the elimination of transitions, a meaningful blank space between the shots or lines, the play and acts of redefinition that occur through the juxtaposition of similar or opposite images—what Pound called the ideogrammic method.

The second national appearance in print by "Mr. George A. Oppen of Belvedere, California" (after the "Objectivists" issue of *Poetry*) was again in *Poetry*, January 1932. Four poems under the title "Discrete Series," only one of which was to be reprinted in the volume two years later. The second reads:

> When, having entered—
>
> Your coat slips smoothly from your shoulders to the waiter:
>
> How, in the face of this, shall we remember,
> Should you stand suddenly upon your head
>
> Your skirts would blossom downward
>
> Like an anemone.

Inversion, incongruity, contradiction. It should be said, once, that Oppen can be very funny. (In conversation, gnomic one-liners alternate with ironic anecdotes, all punctuated by a bobbing of those unavoidable eyebrows: a gesture that might have been stolen from Groucho Marx.) An Oppen line and a joke are, at times, structurally identical: giving "expression to a whole characteristic by means of a tiny detail," so that "where we might have expected something new, something familiar is rediscovered" (Freud). The tension of the minute or the irrelevant, seen in terms of its potential or actual effect: in comedy, the banana peel; in tragedy, Richard II's and Oppen's "little pin."

Objectivism as a topic, or as an approach to Oppen, could be permanently retired. Oppen has one poem, nine lines, in the 200-odd pages of *An "Objectivists" Anthology*. The book and the *Poetry* issue preclude taxonomy. The Objectivists included, besides the Oppen-Rakosi-Reznikoff-Zukofsky quaternity, Williams, Rexroth, Bunting, Mary Butts, McAlmon, Eliot, Charles Henri Ford, Parker Tyler, John Wheelwright, Samuel Putnam, Norman MacLeod, Emmanuel Carnevali, Ezra Pound (represented by his worst poem, "der yiddisher Charleston Band") and—Arthur Rimbaud. Forgotten Objectivists include Howard Weeks, S. Theodore Hecht, Henry Zolinsky, Harry Roskolenkier, Jesse Lowenthal, Richard Johns, Martha Champion, Joyce Hopkins, Frances Fletcher, Forrest Anderson, and R. B. N. Warriston. Lorine Niedecker was not an Objectivist. The most famous Objectivist is Whittaker Chambers.

What links the poets is that all were contacted by the editor, Zukofsky. Only a few of their contributions are possibly "objectivist." Of the four poets now known as "Objectivists," there is only one statement (biographical or aesthetic) which is applicable to all: They were Jewish, and they were obscure at the time.

Because of his silence, Oppen is (with César Vallejo) the only Communist Party poet who never wrote doggerel. That silence is both admirable and regrettable, given the few interesting American poets involved in some form of radical politics in the 1930's: Rukeyser, Rexroth, Patchen, Fearing, Hughes. One imagines that Oppen, more than anyone, would have been able to transcend paean and philippic. His poetry from that period remains one of the great unwritten works.

Like Wyatt, a favorite poet, Oppen was a soldier—the only major twentieth-century American poet to participate in combat. Walter Benjamin: "Was it not noticeable at the end of the war that men returned from the battlefield grown silent—not richer, but poorer in communicable experience? . . . For never has experience been contradicted more thoroughly than strategic experience by tactical warfare, economic experience by inflation, bodily experience by mechanical warfare, moral experience by those in power. A generation that had gone to school on a horse-drawn streetcar now stood under the open sky in a countryside in which nothing remained unchanged but the clouds, and beneath these clouds, in a field of force of destructive torrents and explosions, was the tiny, fragile human body."

Like Wyatt, a political exile. And, like many of the best American poets, a literary exile: Oppen has given few readings, has written one book review, has served on no (literary) committees. ". . . one may honorably keep/ His distance/ If he can." With the discovery of that "honorably," Oppen could break his twenty-five-year silence.

Oppen constructs a poem as a mason builds a wall. A line is written, and rewritten by gluing a strip of paper over it. A final manuscript page is, in the end, quite thick. Not coincidentally, a frequent Oppen image is Kafka's wall: both the sum of all human endeavor in one particular culture and that which separates that culture from the others. Oppen's metropolis consists of walls within walls: the Great Wall becomes the Forbidden City. Yet among the walls, Oppen's eye, characteristically, picks a brick.

Oppen: "*Of Being Numerous* asks the question whether or not we can deal with humanity as something which actually exists." Brecht: "We'd all be human if we could."

Defoe's Crusoe and Oppen's have little in common. Oppen takes the fact of shipwreck, the beginning of the myth (though not of the novel) and ignores the capitalist microcosm the sexless colonialist creates. Oppen takes *Robinson Crusoe* for the same reason that Rousseau selects the novel as the one essential book for Emile's education: "The surest way to raise oneself above prejudices, and order one's judgment on the real relationship between things, is to put oneself in the place of an isolated man, and to judge of everything as that man would judge of them according to their actual usefulness."

A clipping, undated (1969?) from the letters to the editor page of *Playboy* magazine. Concerning the publication of Mao Zedong's poetry, George Oppen of San Francisco, California, writes: ". . . The piece as a whole—poems and accompanying commentary—gives some inkling of the way in which poetry is deeply involved in a politics that is radical enough to ask questions of purposes and desires. You are to be applauded for publishing *Seven Poems*. Maybe human voices will wake us before we drown." It is a configuration to ponder: Oppen, Hefner, Eliot, Mao.

Like Wyatt and another favorite, Blake, the juncture of eroticism and the transformation of the social order. It should be said, a few times, that Oppen is a sensualist, author of erotic lyrics of great beauty, rare in English in this century. The great modern love poems in the language are all written by old men and women: "Asphodel," "Briggflatts," "In A Cornish Garden," "Winter Love," "The Love Songs of Marichiko," "Anniversary Poem."

Theodor Lipps, cited by Freud: "A joke says what it has to say, not always in few words, but in *too* few words—that is, in words that are insufficient by strict logic or by common modes of thought and speech. It may even actually say what it has to say by not saying it." For the word "joke," substitute the phrase "Oppen's later poetry."

Most modern poems require a pause at line's end. With silence in the right- and left-hand margins, the poem becomes a brick amidst nothing. The later Oppen poems usually employ a pause in the middle of the line: the poem is a cylinder, enclosing silence. The still center, Zukofsky's "total rest." Zhuangzi (via Watson): "You have heard of the knowledge that knows, but you have never heard of the knowledge that does not know. Look into that closed room, the empty chamber where brightness is born." Oppen: "Hopper . . . was very close to us."

Surprisingly, Oppen may be the only major English-language poet in the century to write exclusively from his own experience. No personae, no mythology, no foreign words, no translation, one or two passing historical references, a handful of literary allusions, no exotica, no surrealism, no documentary collage. Oppen, then, stands apart from them all: H. D., Pound, Yeats, Eliot, Rexroth, Williams, MacDiarmid, Stevens, David Jones, Hughes, Crane, Bunting—and even from Reznikoff, Zukofsky, Niedecker.

Direct experience, the life of one mind, transformed word by word—less than 300 pages of work in 50 years—into an unadorned yet radiant speech. In a society where the economy is based on extravagance, economy can only seem austere. Thus Oppen as "minimalist," an utterly inappropriate badge. Octavio Paz, reading the four-line section 22 of "Of Being Numerous," remarked: "This is very beautiful. But in Spanish one would not have to use so many words."

O small ones, small lawns of home, the little seed eyes, little seed, little violent, diligent seed, little sparrow, round and sweet, so little said of it, the dangling small beast, the small towns, little solitude, the small black tugs, small harbors, the small rains, blue waves roughly small, the little core of oneself, small like a small hawk, the little landing places, small embarkation points, the small beauty of the forest, the alien small teeth, the small nouns, the small resorts of the small poor, the little hole in the eye, the little hole, the smallest corners of man's triumph, o small boy, the very small coves, the little boat, these small stony worlds, these small worlds, the small prows of the fish boats, the little grain, the little bulbs, the houses small as in the skulls of birds, small hollow in the flesh, a little life, sprouting little green buds, the small trees, the small doors, so small a picture, small objects of wood and the bones of fish and of stone, the little woods, let it be small enough, a small room, small self-interest, the small mid-ocean, these little dumps, the homes of small animals, small blazing sun of the farms, the cliffs small and numerous, the little skirts, cold little pin unresting, small pin of the wind and the rayne, the small paved area, the rain's small pellets, small fountains, her small voice among the people, the small selves haunting us in the stones, in their small distances the poem begins, thru the airs small very small alien, joy in the small huge dark, the glory of joy in the small huge dark:

Coleridge: ". . . the universe itself—what but an immense heap of *little* things?"

[1980]

A Spook in the House of Poetry

1901: It had been a difficult birth; the mother had almost died. Perhaps in revenge, she insisted that he be given a girl's name: Vivian. His father, an illustrator, a sort of lowbrow bohemian, dressed at home in a kimono and rarely spoke. With the birth of a second child, Dickie, the family moved to a village on Long Island. Their large crumbling house was without heat; leaks there went unrepaired for decades. Neighbors shunned them as exotics. They were assumed to be French.

After the father abandoned them for a male lover, the mother and the two boys would sleep together in a locked room, a bureau pushed against the door; she with an axe by her bed, Vivian with a knife under his pillow. He would remember afternoons, lying on a couch with an unattended toothache, staring at a print on the wall: a beckoning skeleton, captioned "Death the Comforter."

Some years later the father returned to live in the house like John Gabriel Borkman, silently, entirely apart from the family. Meals were brought to his room on a tray. One morning he walked out and, without a word, hacked up the flowers.

The boy amused himself by taking long walks in the woods, learning French, German, Spanish, Latin, Greek, and dabbling in Hindustani, Persian, Gaelic, Romany, Russian, and the Assyrian cuneiform inscriptions. He wrote: "I am an outcast. My family is outcast. We have no friends, no social ties, no church, no organization that we claim and that claims us, no community." It is the childhood of a poet, a criminal, an ideologue, a spy, a closet homosexual, a scholar, or an informer.

Vivian was to be all of these. He enters the public domain in 1920 when, after drifting around the country, he took his mother's maiden name as his own and enrolled at Columbia University as Whittaker Chambers.

At Columbia, Chambers discovered poetry, inspired by an enthusiastic instructor, Mark Van Doren (then working on his first book) and fellow students Louis Zukofsky, Clifton Fadiman, Langston Hughes, Lionel Trilling. There too he discovered Communism. Zukofsky, for one, lent him a copy of the *Manifesto*. In 1923, when Chambers was forced out of school for publishing an atheistic play in the college magazine, Van Doren suggested he go to the new Soviet Union. He went instead to Europe with a student of art history, Meyer Schapiro.

Back from a short Grand Tour, he worked at the New York Public Library until he was dismissed for stealing books. His lovers were men or married women. His best friend was Zukofsky. He lived at home, or occasionally in a tent on the beach with a boyfriend. Home consisted of his mutually isolated parents, an insane grandmother who wandered the house with a knife in her hand, and an increasingly disturbed Dickie, who alternated suicidal depressions with wild nights cruising the speakeasies.

His concerns were poetry and Communism. The poems, published in *The Nation* from 1924 to 1926, are moody, self-consciously "modern," and sometimes cruel. In one, "Quag-Hole," the narrator arrives at a rendezvous outside of town. He hides; a woman appears; he watches her wait for him for hours; she leaves; he leaves. Another, an untitled poem on pears, ends abruptly:

> . . . Where heels have ground
> The pears to pulp late bees and yellow
> Wasps fly fiercely: some are drowned.

There is one homoerotic poem, "Tandarei," published by the avant-garde pornographer Samuel Roth in his magazine *Two Worlds*. Steamy perhaps for 1926, it finally may say more than it intends:

> But all my hand can encompass and possess
> Is the tiny spinal-cords in your neck, and the ribs that drop
> So fearfully into the cavity when you press
> On me your heart that seems, at moments to make full stop,
> As your sap drains into me in excess,
> Like the sap from the stems of a tree that they lop.

> And, as you draw your limbs like a pale
> Effulgence around me, I must
> Have them drawn into me,—as you fail
> And begin to leave me. You shall be a hand thrust
> Into my flesh; your hand thrust into me impale
> My flesh forever on yours, driven in thru body-crust.

It ends, a page later:

> Now I am right
> In what I offended,
> I may go go forth again, again unmastered, into the light.

Chambers joined the Party in 1925, to the dismay, he claimed, of his "fellow traveler" intellectual friends. One of them, undoubtedly Zukofsky, was recalled twenty-seven years later in Chambers' ponderous autobiography, *Witness*: "I told him the news. As usual, he squinted one eye and lifted the eyebrow of the other, so that he looked as if he were peering through a monocle. 'Do you drill in a cellar with machine guns?' he asked airily."

In 1926, after a number of suicide attempts thwarted by Whittaker at the last moment, Dickie Chambers was found dead, his head resting on a pillow stuck in an oven. Zukofsky commemorated him in "Poem Beginning 'The'" (lines 76–129) and, two years later, in one of the most beautiful elegies of the century, the third movement of "*A*", which begins:

> *At eventide, cool hour*
> Your dead mouth singing,
>
>   Ricky . . .

By 1930, Chambers had become mildly famous as the translator of a bestseller, Felix Salton's *Bambi*, of all things, and as the author of poems in *The Daily Worker* and short stories in *The New Masses*. The poems were routine ("For the dead, the dead, the dead, we march, comrades, workers") but the stories were a success: Lincoln Steffens praised them, the Moscow magazine *International Literature* found their questions "correctly" raised, and they were dramatized and translated in odd corners of the world. The next year Zukofsky included Chambers in the "Objectivists" issue of *Poetry*. His poem, also on Dickie's death, begins:

> The moving masses of clouds, and the standing
> Freights on the siding in the sun, alike induce in us
> That despair which we, brother, know there is no withstanding.

and continues in a similarly abstract vein: "Only motionlessness as of the cars,/ In beings of substance, remains undemeaning." On the preceding page is "1930's" by George A. Oppen (later to become part of *Discrete Series*); on the following page, "The Word" by Basil Bunting.

After brief service as the editor of *The New Masses*, Chambers left literature in 1932 to join a society even more obscure and elite than those of poetry, Party, and unspoken sexuality: the Fourth Section of Soviet Military Intelligence. He was never again a poet; as a spy he seems to have done little of importance.

In 1948 he enters history and legend, almost a figure of the contemporary existential fiction: the distasteful martyr, the outcast messenger bearing—depending on the auditor—false or bad news. His darkly motivated tales of pumpkins and rugs have never been explained. Only their effect is known: they destroyed the government career of one ambitious young man, Alger Hiss, and launched another, Richard Nixon.

During the trials, Chambers gave Zukofsky's name as a character reference. The poet, luckily, never testified, but the *Poetry* issue was entered as evidence. It is a moment to imagine in the history of modernism: the young Congressman Nixon, puzzling over pages of Objectivist verse.

Of Zukofsky's once "beautiful/ Almost sexual// Brothers," Whittaker Chambers has frozen in the mind as, in his own words, "the short, squat, solitary figure, trudging through the impersonal halls of public buildings to testify before Congressional committees, grand juries, loyalty boards, courts of law." In the last year of his life, he was writing his friend William F. Buckley of his love for Lorca.

[1981]

Langston Hughes

Langston Hughes is still probably the world's best-known black writer. Yet his reputation, nearly twenty years after his death, is in name only: most of the work is out of print, and the little available is little read, especially by whites. Hughes, more than anyone, is representative of a few facts of American reading and writing life:

—White people generally do not read books by black writers.

—White people tend to read books by black writers only during those periods when particularly overt repression (the 1919 riots, the 1950's desegregation violence) has led to black militancy and white liberal sympathy (the early 1920's, the early 1960's). [South African writers have experienced similar waves of indifference and literary interest in the U.S.]

1925 is an emblematic year. Hughes was only twenty-three, yet he had already published some of his most famous poems, such as "The Negro Speaks of Rivers" and the poem that begins, "I, too, sing America." He had lived with his errant father in Mexico, had traveled extensively through western Africa as a merchant seaman, had worked in Montmartre as a doorman and dishwasher.

The America of 1925 was a country where, in the North, it was considered liberal to have black domestic servants; where blacks could not eat at downtown restaurants; where black playwrights could not buy orchestra seats to see their own plays on Broadway. Among the white intelligentsia, however—the Party people and the party people—everything black was the rage: jazz, African art, Afro-American folklore, Harlem nightlife. Typically, in 1925, Hughes' first book was about to be published by Knopf, *Vanity Fair* was printing his poems, and the only job he could get was as a busboy in a Washington D.C. hotel.

The reaction to that first book, *The Weary Blues* (published

the following year), exemplifies much of the continuing reception of black writing in this country. One thrust of the Harlem
Renaissance of the 1920's had been to write poetry that, while
incorporating some black material, would generally be acceptable to whites—to prove that blacks could write as well as whites,
playing by white rules. Countee Cullen, for example, claimed
Keats as his "god" and Edna St. Vincent Millay his "goddess";
Claude McKay wrote militant poetry couched in traditional verse
forms. Hughes, however, attempted to write in the spoken language of the streets, tossing classical prosody out the window in
favor of jazz rhythms. The title poem of his book ended:

> The stars went out and so did the moon.
> The singer stopped playing and went to bed.
> While the Weary Blues echoed through his head.
> He slept like a rock or a man that's dead.

The Weary Blues was generally disliked by black critics at the
time. Cullen wrote, "There is too much emphasis here on strictly
Negro themes." Hughes countered a few months later:

One of the most promising of the young Negro poets said to me
once, "I want to be a poet—not a Negro poet," meaning, "I want
to write like a white poet," meaning, subconsciously, "I would like
to be a white poet," meaning behind that, "I would like to be
white." And I was sorry the young man said that, for no great poet
has ever been afraid of being himself. . . .

Hughes' simple point—that one is simultaneously a black poet
and a poet—has rarely been realized in American letters. There
have always been two traps: on the one hand, in times when
blacks are not in fashion, the white literary establishment likes it
black poets white, writing in received forms with a few "mother-
fuckers," a burnt-out tenement, or a palm tree thrown in for local
color. On the other hand, black poets who write without compromise are seen only as blacks, not as poets. Hughes himself, whose
work in the 1920's toward a writing out of real speech parallels
that of William Carlos Williams, is never mentioned in any
history of American modernism, never juxtaposed in a critical
essay with a white poet. If he appears at all in literary histories, it
is always in the ghetto of a chapter entitled "The Harlem Renais-

sance."* Yet simultaneously, and more or less independently, Hughes was writing work which could easily be mistaken for Reznikoff:

Suicide's Note

The calm,
Cool face of the river
Asked me for a kiss.

or Zukofsky:

Be-Bop Boys

Imploring Mecca
to achieve
six discs
with Decca.

or Williams-like collages of real speech, such as the poem that begins:

Playboy of the dawn,
Solid gone!
Out all night
Until 12—1—2 a.m. . . .

In fact, his extracts of American speech often seem more exact than Williams:

Maybe

I asked you, baby,
If you understood—
You told me that you didn't
But you thought you would.

After 1929, the Negro was no longer in vogue: the whole world

---

*Worse, the continuing ghettoization of writers like Hughes has been fostered not only by the white establishment, but also by black scholars in the universities: Today a Williams belongs to the English Dept., but a Hughes can only be found in Black Studies. University departments are fiercely territorial, and the result of what initially was meant to redress an imbalance is that black writers now belong exclusively to Black Studies, women writers to Women's Studies, and the English Dept., as always, remains the province of white males.

had become black. Yet it was during the Depression that Hughes not only did much of his best writing, but also gained a world-wide following as he joined the international struggle against the twin evils of the era, fascism and capitalism.

In 1931, the year the Scottsboro Boys went on trial, Hughes spent nine months traveling 36,000 miles of American back roads in an old jalopy, lecturing and reading at schools and community centers, evading hecklers and pickets. [One of his essays on the experience is called "On the Road"; like Kerouac, he could not drive.] In 1932 he left for the Soviet Union to work on a disastrous film project about race relations in the U.S. He stayed a year, touring everywhere, writing for American and Soviet newspapers and translating Russian writers. It was "the only place I've ever made enough to live from writing." Hughes was feted throughout the country—a black in the U.S.S.R. was more exotic than a Cotton Club show. But for Hughes it was his first, and only, glimpse of a world without racism. He wrote: "Put one more S in the USA."

His story is the history of the age. He knew everyone from Tristan Tzara to Ramon Navarro; he hung out with the radical intellectuals in China and in Mexico, was deported from Japan as a spy. He helped lead a farmworkers' strike in Carmel, wrote (unproduced) screenplays in Hollywood, ran a "suitcase" black theater company. He was a war correspondent, and slightly wounded, in the Spanish Civil War. He seemed to be everywhere in the 1930's, at every conference and on every petition, all the while producing an astonishing heap of poems, articles, plays, libretti, translations, anthologies, children's books.

Some of his poetry of the period sounded like this:

> White Man! White Man!
> Let Louis Armstrong play it—
> And you copyright it
> And take the money [. . .]
> I hear your name ain't really White Man.
> I hear it's something
> Marx wrote down
> Fifty years ago—
> That rich people don't like to read.

Is that true, White Man?
Is your name in a book
Called the Communist Manifesto?
Is your name spelled
C-A-P-I-T-A-L-I-S-T?
Are you always a White Man?
Huh?

It skirts doggerel, and yet—nothing of the kind was to be heard
again in America for another thirty years. As for that "Huh?"—
the last line of the poem—there's almost nothing like it in American poetry, a moment of rage and disdain transcending speech.

As a Communist, his faith crumbled, with that of so many
others, at the Hitler-Stalin pact. After that, his writing lost its
militancy, and he settled in Harlem as a kind of elder statesman
and cultural center for the younger black artists. He wrote as
much as ever, but only in his last years, as the civil rights
movement picked up, did the work regain its political fervor.

He was hounded through the years by the FBI and by the
House Un-American Activities Committee. Called before
McCarthy, he was a partially "friendly" witness—but one who
refused to name names. The Red-baiting era was also to have an
inadvertently calamitous effect on his reputation: In 1958 and
1959 he edited the *Langston Hughes Reader* and a *Selected
Poems*, retaining some of his civil rights pieces but entirely
eliminating his more militant writing. It was an act of self-
mutilation, understandable at the time—but twenty-five years
later that same *Selected Poems* is the only book of Hughes' poetry
that one can buy. On the basis of that book, Hughes is seen by
younger readers as a folklorist and early advocate of "black is
beautiful"—an important but remote figure. A *Collected Poems*,
if it ever comes, will prove that Hughes' work has the urgency of
the latest poem from Amiri Baraka, that his post-World War I
writing was in the forefront of American modernism, and that
his last major work, *Montage of a Dream Deferred*, deserves
consideration along with the other multivoiced long poems of
the American city: Williams' *Paterson*, Tolson's *Harlem Gallery*,
Long's *Pittsburgh Memorandum*, Sousandrade's *Wall Street In-
ferno*, Crane's *The Bridge*.

Surely it's time that Hughes was taken seriously again:

> What happens
> to a dream deferred:
>
> Daddy, ain't you heard?

[1983]

Another Memory of Charles Reznikoff

Using what is plain and simple he fashioned subtle lines;
Taking the most ordinary words, he changed them into wonders.
—Dai Fu-gu (on Lu Yu)

And he could make music out of the legalistic, the driest of this
reading . . . as a savage can out of sticks and a hide.
—*The Lionhearted*

A few years before Charles Reznikoff died, an organization called
Poetry in Public Places was running outdoor readings in various
parts of town. Reznikoff, aptly, had been asked to read on the
promenade in Brooklyn Heights, by the waters of Manhattan,
looking out to the vertical city. I had arranged to meet him at
Harvey Shapiro's house, a few blocks away, and the three of us
walked over to where the reading was to occur.

When we reached the spot, we discovered that Charles had been
given the wrong date: posters were up announcing the reading
for the following week. But it was a beautiful Sunday afternoon,
the promenade was packed with strollers, and Charles decided to
read anyway. He put his old briefcase on a park bench, stood next
to it, and began to read.

People stopped, as they always do in New York, thinking he
was a local eccentric. But they did not move on. Within fifteen
minutes Charles had an enthusiastic crowd of perhaps a hundred
people, cheering at the end of each poem—the anecdotes of city
life he had had to publish himself, near the end of his long life, in
an edition of two hundred copies.

It was a sweet moment. Reznikoff was, in this century, the
great poet of New York. Someday there will be a plaque on West

End Avenue, and a library branch named after him. But he was a populist poet with no public, writing a poetry that could speak to anyone, but rarely did.

A man who walked ten to twenty miles a day in the city, he was the perfect passer-by: all eyes, all ears, and forever speechless. His is the poetry of the passer-by, a phenomenon that begins with Baudelaire's "I might have loved you, and you knew it!" [which Reznikoff would have written as, "I might have loved you, or might not have, but you didn't know it"] and includes, among so many others, Williams' woman in slacks in *Paterson V*, much of Lorca's *Poet in New York*, and this Reznikoffian couplet from a Mexican, José Juan Tablada, fifty years ago:

> You women who walk on Fifth Avenue,
> So close to my eyes, so far from my life.

That afternoon in Brooklyn Heights, the Passer-by was at last, at eighty, after a life of—imposed or self-imposed?—silence, speaking to the other passers-by. I recall the day for one reason: it is the only untold Reznikoff story I know that doesn't end with one of Charles' wry but finally maddening, self-deprecating remarks.

I wrote him wildly enthusiastic letters, soliciting work for a magazine I edited, *Montemora*, offering him as many pages as he liked. The manuscripts he sent in reply always contained a self-addressed stamped envelope. Yet this invisible man, who published his own books for fifty years, who never left the country, who sat through the Casbah of Hollywood in the 1930's watching the flies on his desk, whose poetry is filled with people but no friends, who rarely mentioned in print his life after late adolescence or his wife of forty-six years—this man also lived in the world of *Testimony, Holocaust, The Lionhearted,* the novel *By the Waters of Manhattan*: It was a world of injustice without ultimate justice, of disembodied outbursts of violent passion, of suffering without the illusion of a political or spiritual redemption. If Reznikoff's life is ever known, I suspect that what we saw as an untiring humility will be far more tragic.

[1983]

Octavio Paz

Mexico, perhaps more than China, is the Middle Kingdom. In the current political moment, its centrality lies on a north-south axis: for North Americans, as the relatively stable, partially friendly buffer state between "us" and the turmoil we misunderstand in Central America; for Mexicans, as a nation placed between the closing jaws of Northern imperialism and Southern revolt.

Historically, however, Mexico was a Middle Kingdom between the oceans, between East and West. Before the arrival of Cortéz in 1519 the country was, it seems likely, the eastern edge of a transpacific cultural network—China, Japan, and India; Polynesia; Mexico, Peru, and Ecuador—one that will never be fully known, but which is apparent in various artworks across the ocean. With Cortéz, of course, Mexico became the western end of the Spanish Empire, with a European language and religion, and with a government no more enlightened than its Aztec predecessor.

There is a navel (*xi*, in Nahuatl) in the middle of the word Mexico, and the navel of the Middle Kingdom was the city Tenochtitlán, today's Mexico City, built literally on the water, but facing no sea. It was the capital of an empire that radiated from its ring of volcanoes and pyramids: an expanding self-absorbed sun, devoted to feeding, with art and blood, the other, celestial sun.

Mexico—a xenophobe whom strangers won't leave alone—has been the center of a global mandala. It is this configuration that Octavio Paz has, in his life and in the work, traced to its furthest reaches. A great synthesizer, he has transformed the picture while simultaneously drawing his own self-portrait.

Born in a suburb of Mexico City in 1914, Paz began at the center and followed the Mexican mandala in three directions. East: as a young Marxist to the Spanish Civil War, and as a

surrealist to Paris in the late 1940's. North: to San Francisco and
New York during the Second World War, and in the 1970's to
various American universities. West: to China and Japan in 1952,
and as the Mexican ambassador to India from 1962 to 1968.

From the U.S. he gained a vision of overdevelopment and a
view of his own country on the outskirts of history: the pathos of
its nationalistic ardor. From Europe, the belief in poetry as "the
secret religion of the modern age"; that the revolution of the
word is the revolution of the world, and that both cannot exist
without a revolution of the body: life as art, a return to the
mythic lost unity of thought and body, man and nature, I and the
other. From India, and his studies of Buddhism and Tantrism,
the revelation of passion binding the world in illusion, and of
passion as the liberator of the world: that in the moment of
passion's self-negation, the world dissolves, "transparency is all
that remains."

He is "a man in love with silence who can't stop talking," a
restless mind, forever curious, in seemingly perpetual motion.
There is something Aztec in this, despite that society's bloody
singlemindedness and rigidity: In Nahuatl, the artist is *tlayol-
teuanni*, he who sees with his heart. Heart, *yollotl*, comes from
the word movement, *ollin*. At the tops of temples, living hearts
were cut out to feed the sun, to keep it moving. Time was a
turning wheel, the familiar sunstone. For the Aztecs, the great
terror was stasis—that the sun, time, the world would stop. Paz's
mobility, though of course the product of an individual tempera-
ment, oddly fits the ancient scheme. Had he been born in Tenochtitlán, he might have been one of the poet-princes, but I
imagine him as a *pochteca*, one of that mysterious band of
pilgrims who wandered the empire in search of the "Land of the
Sun."

Paz is generally read as Latin America's great surrealist poet—
that is, as an exotic European. Yet he remains inherently Mexican, despite the fact that he has always been a cosmopolitan,
never a regionalist or an indigenist. Like the hero of a Sufi
parable, Paz traveled abroad to find what was always at home. He
discovered synesthesia in Rimbaud's colored vowels, not in the
Aztec "painted songs." He practiced dissolving the poet's ego
through automatic writing and Japanese renga, but he came

from a tradition that did not distinguish between poet and poem, where a poet could declare, "God has sent me as a messenger./ I am transformed into a poem."

The famous last line of his "Hymn Among the Ruins," "words that are flowers that are fruits that are acts," could have been written equally by a surrealist or by a member of the Aztec Brotherhood of poets. In the Nahuatl lyric form called *xopan-cuicatl*, a celebration of life and of cyclical time, the poet and the poem become a plant that grows with the poem; the plant becomes the fibers of the book in which the poem is painted; and the fibers of the book become the woven fiber of the mat, the symbol of worldly power and authority. Paz's preoccupation with pairs is also strangely Nahuatl: The Aztecs tended to describe the world by two aspects—poetry was *flower and song*, fame *mist and smoke*, pleasure *wind and heat*—"so that," as Angel Garibay writes, "through the union of these two will come a spark which will bring understanding."

His great Tantric poem *Blanco* owes much to Mallarmé and to Pound's ideogrammic method—each image self-contained and discrete, understood (like the Chinese ideogram itself) only in relation to the other lines, written and unwritten; each a centripetal force drawing the other images and meanings toward it, an implosion that leads to the explosion of the poem. Yet *Blanco* was also designed as an Aztec book, a folded screen. Those screens of painted songs, images rather than script, were "read" as mnemonic devices: the reader created the text, the text created itself, as *Blanco* with its variant readings intends.

The surrealists sought a way out of European rationalism and bourgeois capitalist values by recovering their own archaic history and by immersing themselves in the surviving indigenous cultures of the world. Paz, on a similar quest—to free himself from the straitjacket of ex-colonial provincialism, that child more orthodox than its parent—went to Europe to discover the other, heretical and subterranean, European tradition. It is an irony of the age: while Paz was writing on de Sade and Fourier, his friend the French poet Benjamin Péret was translating the Mayan *Book of the Chilam Balam of Chumayel*.

The surrealist motto—"liberty, love and poetry"—applies in varying degrees to most of the modernists of the first half of the century: women and men dedicated to the imagination, to social revolution, to the transformation of all the arts, to the integration of life and art. It seems incredible that that era has passed, that we have entered an age of specialized arts practitioners. Surely others will come, but at the moment Paz is among the last of the poets who drew their own maps of the world.

[1983]

At the Death of Kenneth Rexroth

It's a typical story: I was assigned, at my suggestion, to write an obituary on Kenneth Rexroth for *The Nation*, a magazine he had served for fifteen years as San Francisco correspondent. Written in the week after his death, the article was promptly rejected for "overpraising a minor writer" (and a "sexist pig" to boot). The obituary was then sent, at the recommendation of Carol Tinker, Rexroth's widow, to the *American Poetry Review*. Two months later they replied that they would be happy to run the piece sometime next year, and would I please send a photograph of myself to accompany it? Considering their leisure, and my mug, inappropriate to the occasion, I withdrew the article. *Sulfur* magazine, just going to press, then offered to add an extra page in the front of their issue—and only there, in the obscure, sometimes honorable domain of the little magazine, could a condensed version of my small notice of Rexroth's death finally see print.

It's a typical story: one cannot even publish an obituary for an American poet, for the best of them die even more forlorn than they lived. In the last twenty-five years, despite the so-called "poetry boom" and the thousands of poetry books published yearly, most of the important American poets have died with most of their work unpublished or out of print. Louis Zukofsky, H. D., Langston Hughes, Paul Blackburn, Charles Olson, Marianne Moore, Mina Loy, Frank O'Hara, Charles Reznikoff, Jack Spicer, Lorine Niedecker, to name a few. The small group who died in print were either approved by the English Dept. in their lifetimes (Frost, Eliot, Lowell, *et al.*) or they appealed to adolescents (Cummings) or they were among the few published and kept in print by New Directions (Pound, Williams, and now Rexroth).

With certain exceptions, the death of an American poet inverts

the reputation. Those who were heavily laureled in their lifetimes seem to vanish from their graves (Tate, Ransom, Teasdale,
MacLeish, Van Doren, Schwartz, Wylie, Bogan, Bynner, Jarrell,
Aiken, Winters, Hillyer, and so many more). For those who were
dismissed or neglected in life, death becomes the primary condition for immortality. The English Dept. is usually too late for the
funeral, but they are enthusiastic exhumers. Their critical appa-
ratus grinds into motion and, often many years later, buoyed by
exegesis, the original at last rises to the surface. Canonization is
complete, and we all too easily assume that those islands were
always on the map. [We've already forgotten that Williams won
his only Pulitzer Prize posthumously and that even in his last
years he was considered by the academicians to be a sort of
Grandma Moses of poetry; that the last volume of the *Cantos* was
deemed unworthy of review anywhere; that H. D. at her death
was remembered only for a handful of her earliest poems and that
it took over twenty years for an edition of her *Collected Poems* to
appear; that Marianne Moore's *Collected* was, until recently, out
of print for seventeen years; that Louis Zukofsky was writing for
thirty-three years before he received a single review or article on
his work.]

Now, with a special issue of *Sagetrieb* ("A Journal Devoted to
the Poets in the Pound-Williams-H. D. Tradition" published by
the University of Maine at Orono) the ivy gates are opening to
admit Mr. Rexroth. People will make a living explaining him,
and the mountains of his life and work will swarm with curios-
ity-seekers, pedants, muck-rakers and axe-grinders, all as tiny as
the figures in a Chinese landscape painting. It's easy to imagine
what Rexroth would have said about them—but what will they
make of Rexroth? How will they take the most readable American poet of the century and render him difficult—that is, requir-
ing explication, better known as "teachable"?

I sit with a pile of clippings: *Poetry* magazine, reviewing
Rexroth's first book, comparing the poems to the license plates
made by convicts, and suggesting that the poet consider another
profession. Alfred Kazin calling him an "old-fashioned American sorehead." *The New Yorker*, with its usual bemused conde-
scension, nicknaming him "Daddy-O." John Leonard in the

New York Times: "He lives in Santa Barbara, Calif., where he professes Buddhism and meditates. Meditates? The heart sinks. If Mr. Rexroth is meditating, then he is not being the curmudgeon of old, of fond memory . . . [the] father figure to the various dandies with black fingernails."

And the obituaries: in New York, "Father Figure to Beat Poets"; in L.A., "Artist and Philosopher." A few days later, the longer assessments: Colman McCarthy, in the *Washington Post*, surprised that the newspaper obituaries "ran no longer than a few inches," but assuming that the "magazines that Rexroth wrote for—*The Nation, Commonweal, Saturday Review, Poetry*—[will] provide the full appreciations that he deserves." (None did.) Herbert Mitgang, in the *New York Times*, declaring with parenthetical snideness that he "will probably be remembered as a public personality and as an inspiration (in some circles) more than as a major poet, critic or painter."

Born in another country, Rexroth would have served as the intellectual conscience of the nation: a Paz, Neruda, MacDiarmid, Hikmet. But here, as he wrote, "There is no place for a poet in American society. No place at all for any kind of poet at all." So in his life, and at his death, he was largely seen as a crank, a colorful American eccentric who once spiced occasional magazine copy and three well-known romans à clef.

It is depressing that a few moments from that vast and protean life were bottled and preserved for use *ad infinitum* whenever the name of Rexroth was mentioned. How sad that he died, in the mind of America, an aged Beatnik. For what is more remote than the Beat Generation? To read *The Dharma Bums* today (where Rexroth appears as a "bow-tied wild-haired old anarchist fud," and which has dated far more than, say, Henry Miller) is to see that the Beats mainly offered an attractive selection of alternative consumer choices—red wine, Chinese food eaten with chopsticks, heterosexual sex without marriage, hitchhiking, a taste for non-representational painting, a serious appreciation of jazz, casual dress, occasional tolerance for gay sex, some dabbling in meditation and Oriental philosophy and the occult, facial hair, marijuana—all of which quickly became the common stuff of middle-class American weekends while, ironically, the Beats continued to retain their "wild Boho" image.

Rexroth briefly embraced the Beats (despite his famous disclaimer, "An entymologist is not a bug") as he had so many movements: the Wobblies, the John Reed Clubs, anarchism, the Communist Party (which refused him membership), civil rights, the hippies, feminism—most of which posed a far more serious threat to institutional America than the Beats. But as a political thinker and activist, he essentially belonged to "the generation of revolutionary hopelessness." More than any other poet, Rexroth's work records that history of disillusionment: the massacre of the Kronstadt sailors, Sacco and Vanzetti, the Spanish Civil War, the Moscow Trials, the Hitler-Stalin pact, Hiroshima. He wrote, in 1957:

> We thought we were the men
> Of the years of the great change,
> That we were the forerunners
> Of the normal life of mankind.
> We thought that soon all things would
> Be changed, not just economic
> And social relationships, but
> Painting, poetry, music, dance,
> Architecture, even the food
> We ate and the clothes we wore
> Would be ennobled. It will take
> Longer than we expected.

Still he clung to the vision of brotherhood exemplified by the various American Utopian communities whose history he wrote. His 1960 essay, "The Students Take Over," was dismissed by an academic critic as "mad" for "announcing a nationwide revolution among students on behalf of national and international integrity." Yet by 1969 *The Nation* would write, "What is most viable in the so-called New Left is in large part the creation of Rexroth and Paul Goodman whether the movement knows it or not." As always in Rexroth's life, the initial reaction stuck while the fact that he was proved right was forgotten: "When a prophet refuses to go crazy, he becomes quite a problem, crucifixion being as complicated as it is in humanitarian America."

His enemies were the institutions (the U.S. and Soviet states, the corporations, the universities, the church) and their products: sexual repression, academic art, racism and sexism, the charmlessness of the bourgeoisie, the myth of progress, the razing of the natural world. He was an early champion of civil rights, and his essays on black life in America are among the few from the period that have not dated. He was the first poet whose enthusiasm for tribal culture was not picked up from Frazer, Frobenius, or the Musée de l'Homme, but rather from long periods of living with American Indians. And he was—almost uniquely among the WASP moderns—not only *not* anti-Semitic, but an expert on Hasidism and the Kabbalah. Most of all, he was America's great Christian poet—a Christianity, that is, which has rarely appeared in this hemisphere: the communion of a universal brotherhood. And he was America's—how else to say it?—great American poet. For Rexroth, alone among the poets of this century, encompasses most of what there is to love in this country: ghetto street-smartness, the wilderness, populist anti-capitalism, jazz and rock & roll, the Utopian communities, the small bands at the advance guard of the various arts, the American language, and all the unmelted lumps in the melting pot.

As a poet, he had begun with "The Homestead Called Damascus," a philosophical dialogue and the only poem worth reading by an American teenager, and then veered off the track into a decade of "Cubist" experiment. Had he remained there—like, say, Walter Conrad Arensberg—he would be remembered as a minor Modernist, less interesting than Mina Loy and far inferior to his French models, Reverdy and Apollinaire. But by the publication of his first book, *In What Hour*, in 1941, Rexroth had abandoned the Cubist fragments of language—while retaining the Cubist vision of the simultaneity of all times and the contiguity of all places—to write in a sparsely adorned American speech. ("I have spent my live striving to write the way I talk.") It was a poetry of direct communication, accessible to any reader, part of Rexroth's communitarian political vision, and personal adherence to the mystical traditions of Christianity (the religion of communion) rather than those of the East (the religions of liberation).

The poetry: political, religious, philosophical, erotic, elegiac; celebrations of nature and condemnations of capitalism. His long poems of interior and exterior pilgrimage are the most readable in English in this century. Though he wrote short lyrics of an erotic intensity that has not been heard in English for three hundred years—worthy of the Palatine Anthology or Vidyakara's *Treasury*—he essentially belonged to the tradition of chanted poetry, not to lyric song. For some critics the poems were musically flat, yet William Carlos Williams claimed that "his ear is finer than that of anyone I have ever encountered." The way to hear Rexroth is the way he read: to jazz (or, in the later years, koto) accompaniment. The deadpan voice playing with and against the swirling music: mimetic of the poetry itself, one man walking as the world flows about him.

Curiously, his effect on poetry in his lifetime was not as a poet, but as a freelance pedagogue and tireless promoter, as energetic and inescapable as Pound: organizer of discussion groups and reading series and radio programs; responsible for bringing Levertov, Snyder, Rothenberg, Duncan, Tarn, Antin, Ferlinghetti, and others to New Directions; advocate journalist, editor, and anthologist. Though it is difficult to imagine Gary Snyder without Rexroth or Ginsberg's "Howl" without the example of "Thou Shalt Not Kill"; though everyone has read the Chinese and Japanese translations; it seems that few, even among poets, have read "The Phoenix and the Tortoise," "The Dragon and the Unicorn," "The Heart's Garden, The Garden's Heart," "On Flower Wreath Hill," or more than a scattering of the short poems.

The result is that Rexroth at his death was among the best known and least read of American poets. It is a sad distinction that he shares, not coincidentally, with the poet he most resembles, Hugh MacDiarmid. (I speak of MacDiarmid's reputation outside of Scotland.) Except for MacDiarmid's orthodox Marxism and Rexroth's heterodox Christianity, which are mutually exclusive, both were practitioners of short lyrics and long discursive and discoursive poems, both were boundless erudites, and both are formed out of the conjunction of twentieth-century science, Eastern philosophy, radical politics, heterosexual eroticism, and close observation of the natural world. (The resemblance, strangely, went beyond intellectual affinity: Rexroth claimed that he was often mistaken for MacDiarmid in the streets of Edinburgh.)

I suspect that the neglect of Rexroth and MacDiarmid is due to the fact that both are, at heart, outside of (despite their varying sympathies for) the "Pound-Williams-H. D. tradition." Their spiritual grandfathers were Wordsworth and Whitman: the life of the mind on the open road. [It is, by the way, how one writes the Chinese *dao* (*tao*): the character for "head" over the character for "road."] MacDiarmid may have been sunk by his galactic vocabulary, but Rexroth? One guess is that Rexroth was ignored because, by writing poetry that anyone who reads can read, he subverted the system, the postwar university-literary complex. Poets, especially the advance guard, driven to the fringes of society, have developed an unspoken cultishness: a secret fidelity to the "unacknowledged legislator" myth and a tendency toward private languages that are mutually respected rather than shared. The university professors, for their part, enjoy the power of ferreting out the sources and inside information, being the holders of the keys and the decoder rings—playing George Smiley to the poet's Karla. Rexroth blew the circuits by presenting complex thought in a simple language. The English Dept. has no use for "simple" poets, and the Creative Writing School no use for complex thought. He remained an unpinned butterfly.

Nevertheless, there is no question that American literary history will have to be rewritten to accommodate Rexroth, that postwar American poetry is the "Rexroth Era" as much (and as little) as the earlier decades are the "Pound Era." And it will have to take into account one of the more startling transformations in American letters: that Rexroth, the great celebrant of heterosexual love (and for some, a "sexist pig") devoted the last years of his life to becoming a woman poet.

He translated two anthologies of Chinese and Japanese women poets; edited and translated the contemporary Japanese woman poet Kazuko Shiraishi and—his finest translation—the Song Dynasty poet Li Qingzhao (Li Ch'ing-chao); and he invented a young Japanese poet named Marichiko, a woman in Kyoto, and wrote her poems in Japanese and English.

The Marichiko poems are particularly extraordinary. The text is chronological: in a series of short poems, the narrator longs for, sometimes meets, dreams of and loses her lover, and then grows old. Although Marichiko is identified as a "contemporary woman," only two artifacts of the modern world (insecticide and pachinko games) appear in the poems; most of the imagery is pastoral and the undressed clothes are traditional. The narrator is defined only in relation to her lover, and of her lover we learn absolutely nothing, including gender. All that exists is passion:

> Your tongue thrums and moves
> Into me, and I become
> Hollow and blaze with
> Whirling light, like the inside
> Of a vast expanding pearl.

It is America's first Tantric poetry: through passion, the dissolution of the world (within the poem, the identities of the narrator and her lover, and all external circumstances; outside the poem, the identity of Marichiko herself) and the final dissolution of passion itself:

> Some day in six inches of
> Ashes will be all
> That's left of our passionate minds,
> Of all the world created
> By our love, its origins
> And passing away.

The Marichiko poems, together with the Li Qingzhao translations, are masterworks of remembered passion. Their only equal in American poetry is the late work of H. D., "Hermetic Definition" and "Winter Love"—both writers in their old age, a woman and a man as woman. Man as woman: a renunciation of identity, a transcendence of self. As Pound recanted the *Cantos* and fell into silence; as Zukofsky ended "*A*" by giving up the authorship of the poem; Rexroth became the *other*.

Pound left us, in Canto 120, with a vision of paradise and the despair of one who cannot enter paradise. Zukofsky left us with a black hole, *80 Flowers*, an impossible density that few will ever attempt to penetrate. And now Rexroth, speaking through the mask of Li Qingzhao, has left us with passion and melancholy, the ecstasies of one woman (man) in a world seemingly forever on the verge of ruin:

Red lotus incense fades on
The jeweled carpet. Autumn
Comes again. Gently I open
My silk dress and float alone
On the orchid boat. Who can
Take a letter beyond the clouds?
Only the wild geese come back
And write their ideograms
On the sky under the full
Moon that floods the West Chamber.
Flowers, after their kind, flutter
And scatter. Water after
Its nature, when spilt, at last
Gathers again in one place.
Creatures of the same species
Long for each other. But we
Are far apart and I have
Grown learned in sorrow.
Nothing can make it dissolve
And go away. One moment,
It is on my eyebrows.
The next, it weighs on my heart.

[May 1983]

Reading El Salvador

1

In El Salvador, in peaceful times, a favored pastime of the rich was football played on horseback. In place of a ball, they used a live duck.

Five million people once lived there. Today, half a million have fled abroad. The rest are being decimated at the rate of 10,000 political deaths a year.

The left tends to murder soldiers and individuals: high-placed officials and low-placed "informers." The right prefers the murder of guerrillas, reformers, liberals, and whole villages of peasants, the "sympathizers."

The people are among the hungriest in the hemisphere. It is estimated that a family needs $533 a year for minimal survival; 60% make less. 96.3% of the rural population does not own enough land to support a family. 2% of the population controls 60% of the land.

The last honest elections were held in 1931. After nine months, the government was overthrown by one General Maximiliano Hernández Martínez. In 1932, on a night when volcanoes were erupting throughout Central America, there was a peasant revolt against the General. It failed, and Martínez responded by killing some 25,000 people: *la matanza*, the massacre. He ruled for a dozen more years, holding seances in the palace.

The General would lecture the people over the radio: "Biologists have only discovered five senses. But in reality there are ten. Hunger, thirst, procreation, urination, and defecation are the senses not included in the lists of the biologists." Or, "It is a greater crime to kill an ant than a man, for a man who dies is reincarnated while an ant dies forever." "In El Salvador," he declared, "I am God." During an epidemic, he forbade medical

measures and refused the help of health organizations. Street-
lamps were wrapped in colored cellophane: it was the General's
belief that colored light would purify the air, ending the pestilence.

In 1969, the Honduran Minister of Foreign Affairs stated that
the Colgate toothpaste manufactured in El Salvador was causing
cavities in the teeth of Honduran children. The next day, El
Salvador's Under-Secretary for Economic Integration charged
that Glostura, a hair cream made in Honduras, was giving Salvadorans dandruff. Soon after, El Salvador defeated Honduras in
the semifinals for the World Cup. War broke out, killing 2000
soldiers and an unknown number of civilians.

The nominal government of El Salvador is a shifting cast of
military juntas and ephemeral coalition juntas, supported by—
in the last three years—a billion dollars in U.S. or U.S.-sponsored
multilateral aid. Power is held by the Army, the National Guard,
the National Police, the Treasury Police, and various paramili-
tary organizations and death squads.

On the left there are at least fifty opposition groups. Among
them, the Farabundo Martí Front for National Liberation is not
the Farabundo Martí Popular Forces of Liberation; and the Democratic Nationalist Union is not the National Opposition Union,
which is not the National Democratic Union, which is not the
Popular Democratic Union.

The leaders, left and right, are interchanging and interchange-
able. Most are from the elite. They are related, school chums,
intermarried. Alliances are nervous and always shifting: within
the left, within the right, from left to right, right to left. Of the
two Salvadorans best known in the U.S., José Napoleón Duarte,
the winner-then-loser of the last fraudulent election, is currently
a center-rightist promoted by Reagan, having served as a Communist Party candidate for President, a reformist mayor, and a
participant in a military coup. And Roque Dalton, the guerrilla
poet (who once, like the hero of the von Kleist story, escaped
execution when his prison walls crumbled in an earthquake) was
killed by his own organization in the belief that he was a CIA
agent. Today his assassins are sponsored by the Roque Dalton
Cultural Brigade.

Beneath the swirling rainbow slick of factions and counterfactions, there is the groundswell: the popular movements, organizations of farmers, factory workers, shantytown dwellers. Sharing a common enemy (the Army, the oligarchy) with the leftists, the popular organizations enter into desultory alliances with this and that leftist group, but are represented by none. The left, as so often, is debilitated by Marxist exegesis and its taxonomies of mutual dismissal—adventurism, deviationism, militarism, insurrectionism, revisionism, opportunism—while the right grows stronger.

For the outsider—the reader—El Salvador is a story that cannot be followed. There is no simple incarnation of evil (a Somoza, Batista) nor a group seemingly capable of restoring the nation. It is a war without sides—that is, with scores of sides—without ideology and with no solutions other than the mere ascension to power. There is only the continuing suffering of the people, and the isolated individuals and local groups attempting to alleviate that suffering.

It is a triumph of the demonic. In its torture chambers and in its rococo inventions of mutilation, the powers of El Salvador have perfected an anti-art—the imagination as giver of death—and an anti-poetry where every word is its antonym: In the mornings, nude and headless torsos are found with this note pinned to their flesh: ¡*Viva la Matanza*! Long Live the Massacre!

2

El Salvador has now entered North American poetry in the form of a highly publicized book called *The Country Between Us*, and its author, Carolyn Forché, has been acclaimed as the leading young political poet. Denise Levertov, for one, has declared that Forché is "a poet who's doing what I want to do," and Jacobo Timerman, of all people, has laid this iron wreath on the poet's head: "Latin America needs a poet to replace the man who represented in his writings the beauty, sufferings, fears, and dreams of this continent: Pablo Neruda. Carolyn Forché is that voice." The popularity of the book has placed her among the few social poets currently enjoying a large readership in this country: Levertov, Ginsberg, Snyder, Rich.

Forché, like many poets today, appears to have aggressively

marketed herself. What is curious, a sign of the times (of sorts), is the new image of the political poet she embodies. It is impossible to even glance at *The Country Between Us* without first confronting that image. The cover of the book—a book supposedly written out of the human disaster in El Salvador—is a photograph of the kind usually intended to persuade us to buy pornography or perfume: a misty Extreme Close-Up of an attractive woman, with head tilted, eyes looking dreamily toward the light, full lips slightly parted. It is, of course, a portrait of the author herself.

In previous decades a book such as this would have had a grainy photograph of street violence, or an author with a fierce yet compassionate stare. Today, of course, people like people, especially good-looking people. As evidenced by the *American Poetry Review*, even a poem needs an appealing face to go alongside it. And if one must read about El Salvador, why not let it be packaged in the form of a seductively photographed woman?

It is even stranger to find how little of *The Country Between Us* is actually concerned with El Salvador, that so much has been made of so little. There are twenty-two poems in the book: fourteen on other matters, and only eight in the section titled "In Salvador 1978–1980." Of those eight, only two were written and are located in the country itself (a visit to a prisoner, a dinner with an Army colonel). Three of the others occur in California or Mallorca, where the poet thinks, or talks to people, about El Salvador. Two have no specific location, but were written outside the country (a Nerudesque cry of compassion for guerrilla friends and an elegy for a slain reformer); and one poem occurs probably in Spain and concerns a woman whose husband was murdered in Argentina. Forché's El Salvador, it seems, is more a state of mind than a state. It is the country the author is "in" wherever she is, and—if the book's title is to be understood at all—a barrier of suffering between the poet and her friends, lovers, readers.

The fourteen other poems in the book are written to a formula. Most are addressed in the first person to a friend, lover, or the poet herself; or they are in the voice of a friend/lover speaking to her. They are elegiac, nostalgic, melancholic, filled with references to distant, violent events. Of the fourteen poems: thirteen mention clothes; eleven refer to food; eleven to beverages, partic-

ularly alcoholic beverages; eleven to sex; ten include a place
name, usually foreign; nine have the word "dead" or "death";
eight refer to smoking.

At her worst, Forché is student-profound ("We have, each of
us, nothing./ We will give it to each other.") corny ("we whis-
pered *yes*, there on the intricate/ balconies of breath, overlook-
ing/ the rest of our lives.") annoying (a poem that ends: "If you
read this poem, write to me./ I have been to Paris since we
parted.") or merely vague:

> We spend our morning
> in the flower stalls counting
> the dark tongues of bells
> that hang from ropes waiting
> for the silence of an hour.
> We find a table, ask for *paella*,
> cold soup and wine, where a calm
> light trembles years behind us.

(This last is creative writing school stuff, and one imagines the
exasperated voice of the professor: did you really spend a morning counting clappers? bells "wait" for silence to pass; where is
"where"? and what does the last line mean anyway?)

Typically, the poetry sounds like this (from a poem describing
her room):

> The bundle of army letters
> were sent from Southeast Asia
> during '67, kept near a bottle
> of vodka drained by a woman
> in that same year who wanted
> only to sleep; the fatigues
> were his, it is she
> whom I now least resemble.
> . . .
> Under the bed, a pouch of money:
> *pesetas, dinar, francs*, the coins
> of no value in any other place.
> In the notebooks you will find
> those places: the damp inner thighs,
> the delicate rash left by kisses,

fingers on the tongue, a swallow
of brandy, a fire.
It is all there, the lies
told to myself because of Paris,
the stories I believed in Salvador
and Granada, and every so often
simply the words calling back
a basket of lemons and eggs,
a bowl of olives.

"Paris" and "Granada" are unexplained elsewhere; the Mediterranean is the usual lemons and olives; the sex is strictly *Playboy*, complete with brandy and fire (though the conjunction, in one line, of "fingers on the tongue" and "swallow" is more vomitive than provocative). The two non-descriptive phrases state the following: "The clothes are his but I am different" and "It's impossible to exchange foreign coins." Otherwise, all the bases are swiftly touched in an air of world-weariness: the victim who suffers because of distant events of which she has no part.

The best, and best-known, poem in the book is actually a bit of prose, written in El Salvador:

The Colonel

What you have heard is true. I was in his house. His wife carried a tray of coffee and sugar. His daughter filed her nails, his son went out for the night. There were daily papers, pet dogs, a pistol on the cushion beside him. The moon swung bare on its black cord over the house. On the television was a cop show. It was in English. Broken bottles were embedded in the walls around the house to scoop the kneecaps from a man's legs or cut his hands to lace. On the windows there were gratings like those in liquor stores. We had dinner, rack of lamb, good wine, a gold bell was on the table for calling the maid. The maid brought the green mangoes, salt, a type of bread. I was asked how I enjoyed the country. There was a brief commercial in Spanish. His wife took everything away. There was some talk then of how difficult it had become to govern. The parrot said hello on the terrace. The colonel told it to shut up, and pushed himself from the table. My friend said to me with his eyes: say nothing. The colonel returned with a sack used to bring groceries home. He spilled many human ears on the table. They were like

dried peach halves. There is no other way to say this. He took one
of them in his hands, shook it in our faces, dropped it into a water
glass. It came alive there. I am tired of fooling around he said. As
for the rights of anyone, tell your people they can go fuck themselves. He swept the ears to the floor with his arm and held the last
of his wine in the air. Something for your poetry, no? he said.
Some of the ears on the floor caught this scrap of his voice. Some
of the ears on the floor were pressed to the ground.

What makes it a prose "poem," apparently, are the last two
lines. They nearly wreck it. After such a powerful real-surreal
incident, why does Forché find it necessary to end with a flourish
of writing school whimsey? The first of the two is a "so what"
line: some (not all?) of the ears heard the colonel's final statement. (They didn't, but it would hardly matter if they had.) The
second, unfortunately, has two readings: not only "listening"—
presumably to the sound of distant hordes approaching—but
also "squashed underfoot."

I find it difficult to see Forché as a political poet at all. The
poems are neither illuminations nor artifacts of a political reality, nor are they calls to action. They belong, rather, to the genre
of revolutionary tourism. In the poems Forché meets, talks to,
sleeps with, thinks of individuals involved in political circumstances (as actors or victims) while remaining an outsider herself,
toujours la gringa. In a poem addressed to guerrilla friends, she
writes:

> You will fight
> and fighting, you will die. I will live
> and living cry out until my voice is gone
> to its hollow of earth, where with our
> hands and by the lives we have chosen
> we will dig deeper into our deaths.
> I have done all that I could do.
> Link hands, link arms with me . . .

By blurring the line between participation and observation, we
are meant to believe that the suffering of El Salvador is Forché's
own suffering. The confusion is common among certain tourists
in the Third World, a form of "going native" for those with
pretension to saintliness. But—need it be said?—being back in

L.A. unable to sleep and angry at the sight of Salvadoran produce in the Safeway (as she tells us in another poem) is not the same as being confined to a one meter by one meter by one meter cell, lying curled in your own shit and menstrual blood.

To presume to "link arms," declaring oneself equal, with those who have endured such torment; to speak to people who will be corpses in the morning and claim that you too are digging deep into your own death—if that means anything at all—and that you have done all that you could do: it is more than naïveté or audacity. It is the liberal side of colonialism. The ears on the dinner table are, in the end, just "something" for her poetry, bits of weight collected for a left-wing white man's burden. For Forché, civil war is an emblem of guilt. That many see her as a "voice" of El Salvador is not incredible: She is the kind of political poet produced in the age of the personal crisis.

[October 1982]

The Spider & the Caterpillar

In a recent survey, 90% of American high school students stated that they do not believe in the existence of the future. What was once a philosophical proposition, an aesthetic obsession, has filtered down to become, for the children of the millennium, a reigning truth. Nothing is certain; the sun may not rise tomorrow.

At the moment of doubt, worlds open up, and each fresh report from those strange worlds leads to further doubt. This has been the century of the invention of the personal and collective unconscious, of anthropology, paleontology, of science fiction and scientific cosmological speculation: the creation of thousands of other worlds, terrestrial and extraterrestrial, apparent to the eye of a traveler or beyond the reach of the telescope, buried in the earth, hidden within an unsuspecting mind. It has been the century where physical science and mathematics are built on fundamental contradiction, where the increasingly precise observation and description of the natural sciences leads only to essential inexplicability.

At the moment of doubt, possibilities become limitless—all of them equally impossible. For poetry, the end of certainty has meant, first, that the poem can no longer be a discrete object, the "poem itself," for behind every poem there is another poem (written or unwritten) that contradicts it, and behind that, another poem. The poem is a becoming, not a being; and the poem, breaking out of its isolation, can no longer be contained by the traditional forms. There is no closure: the poem is only a passage leading to another.

Second, it has meant that the poem must be open to everything, and moreover, that everything must come into the poem. Most of the best American poets of the century have demanded the admission of that which was previously excluded: history, economics, found objects, colloquial speech, the works of the Machine Age, the unbeautiful, scientific vocabulary, frank auto-biography, the whole body, non-human species, idiosyncratic prosodies, icons of mass culture, pictographs, glossolalia, the life of the ghetto.

Third, there has been an impatience with isolated subject matter, the Grecian urn or its homely complement, the red wheelbarrow. For in the century of uncertainty, of mass man and the bombardment of images, one can see the world in a grain of sand only if one simultaneously sees the thousands of undressed oiled bodies baking on the beach, the web of their social interactions, the raw sewage pumped into the sea and the contaminated lives of the marine animals, the kiosks with their pink bunnies and rubber ducks, the thumping transistors and careening frisbies, the bumper-to-bumper traffic snaking along the coast. A macrocosm without microcosm: in the poem all ages are contemporaneous, all events synchronous, each thing is itself and the metaphor of something else. [Metaphor: to transfer from one place to another. In Greece the moving vans are labeled META-PHORA.]

Fourth, it has meant a criticism of (and despair over) the inadequacy of language: a sense that the poem has lost the language that speaks it, that the poet must either wrestle the language back to (a temporary) meaning or surrender to meaninglessness, perhaps even revel in meaninglessness.

And yet, despite the hopelessness of existing words and forms, the infinity of pressing subject matter and structural possibilities, the poem has retained its ancient identity as an image of wholeness—or more exactly, an image toward wholeness. The twentieth-century poet is a maker of intricate and beautiful shards who dreams of the golden bowl: not the poem that is, or was, but the poem that should be.

It is a dream that has provoked, among the best poets, a journey. A journey whose path—as there may be no future ahead—can lead only in one direction: back, toward the origins. An uncovering of the past as it lies within, not a nostalgic return. A psychoanalysis of the self and of the species, that the mouth of the snake will finally find its tail, the poem end, and this cycle of history close.

It is of course a mythic and impossible quest. Tragically, it has often led to easy answers: the submission to higher orders (the Church, Eastern or Western; the state religions of Communism and Fascism) or lesser orders (elites, literary movements, reversions to a perceived "tradition"). Often it has led to disorder: the little neuroses, the madnesses and suicides.

An extraordinary poet on this track—and one who has managed to remain resolutely himself—is Clayton Eshleman. Few other contemporary American poets have gone deeper into human history, personal history, and the body itself. Few have invented, as Eshleman has done, the language to carry him.

Ira Clayton Eshleman Jr., born in Indianapolis, Indiana, in 1935, the only child of Gladys and Ira Clayton. It is a Middle American childhood as imagined by a West German filmmaker: his father, deacon of the church and efficiency expert at a slaughterhouse; his mother, the meticulous housewife who forbids her son to play with children who are not Protestant and white, whose parents smoke or drink, whose mothers wear slacks. The boy himself would later be described by the man as "Charlie MacCarthy": a well-scrubbed, well-groomed wooden dummy.

The piano becomes the first window onto a world outside of Indiana. Ira Clayton starts playing at age seven, gives it up in early adolescence under pressure to be a jock, then, at sixteen, discovers bebop: it is the making of a 1950's "white negro." He enters Indiana University in 1953 as a music major, but soon becomes immersed in the world of the Phi Delta Theta fraternity, with its torturers and victims (Actives and Pledges), its Caligulan rites of Hell Week, its saturation bombing of the opposite sex.

In 1957, having bounced in and out of school, he stumbles into poetry, and within a year much of the rest of his life has fallen into place. He edits the university literary magazine, and is in touch with Zukofsky, Creeley, Corman, Duncan, Olson; in New York he meets the poets of his generation, all still in their twenties: Rothenberg, Antin, Kelly, Wakoski, Schwerner, Economou, and, of particular importance, the slightly older Paul Blackburn. He hitchhikes to Mexico—his first experience of the rest of the world—and, in the course of bumming around, happens upon a book of César Vallejo's poetry. A year later he is in Mexico again, translating Neruda's *Residence on Earth*.

He marries in 1961, spends a year in Taiwan, Korea, and Tokyo, and two years in Kyoto, teaching English. In 1965 he and his wife move to Lima, Peru, where he continues his work on Vallejo and edits an ill-fated bilingual magazine, which is suppressed for political reasons before the first issue is published.

Following the birth of their son, the couple move to New York and soon separate. Eshleman is deep into the 1960's: the antiwar movement, Reichian therapy, hallucinogens. In 1967 he founds *Caterpillar*, the major American poetry magazine of the time. In 1969 he meets Caryl Reiter, who becomes his editor, wife, and archetype. *Caterpillar* ends in 1973, to be reborn eight years later in Los Angeles as *Sulfur*—the fourth incarnation of the Magazine. In 1974 Eshleman begins his intensive studies of the Paleolithic caves of France and Spain. In 1978, after nearly twenty years of work, his translation of Vallejo's *Complete Posthumous Poetry* is published, and is soon followed by translations of Artaud, Vladimir Holan, Michel Deguy, and the complete poetry of Aimé Césaire.

It is an American life of the poet in the late twentieth century, full of subterranean explorations and long hours in the fields above. An outline of the life is helpful, for the poetry is full of autobiographical specifics, and the progression of Eshleman's major books has closely followed the course of the life: from the first book, *Mexico & North* (1962) and its early views of the Third World; to *Indiana* (1964), the poet's childhood and early manhood; *Altars* (1971), an artifact of the 1960's; *Coils* (1973), the synthesis of the earlier books and Eshleman's final coming to terms with Indiana; *The Gull Wall* (1975), which breaks out of autobiography to center on Paul Blackburn and a series of personae "portraits"; *What She Means* (1978), an exploration of woman, as incarnated by Caryl Eshleman; and most recently, to *Hades in Manganese* (1981) and, his best book, *Fracture* (1983), the poet's descent into the Paleolithic.

It is a poetry that sees the life of the mind, and the meandering path of the work, as a series of imaginative confrontations with the "other"—other humans, other species, the historical other, the geographical other, the personal other. Encounters without resolution: each an act of a continually revised self-definition, as the Indiana Eshleman—the mid-century, Middle American, middle-class, white Protestant heterosexual male—sets out to wander in a world that denies every Indiana assumption.

The other humans along this path form a quaternity: the Parents (Ira and Gladys Eshleman), the Woman/Wife (Caryl Eshleman), the Master (César Vallejo), the Friend (Paul Blackburn). These are attended by hosts of angels and demons: spirits of creation—Artaud, Van Gogh, Frida Kahlo, Bill Evans, Max Beckmann, Bud Powell, Francis Bacon, among others—and forces of destruction—murderers, torturers, psychopaths. (And typical of Eshleman's work—where each thing flips to its other side—the creative spirits are often victims of self-destruction, the destroyers inadvertent makers of the poem.) Without these others, the I would be the soundless tree falling in the forest: each is a figure of struggle and love, each a mask to be assumed in the stations of the poet's simultaneous dismantling and invention of the ego.

[And here a word should be said about Eshleman's life as translator. Translation is dependent on the dissolution of the translator's ego for the foreign poet to enter the language—a bad translation is the insistent voice of the translator. Eshleman, in such poems as "The Book of Yorunomado" and "The Name Encanyoned River," presents his long apprenticeship to Vallejo in terms of the lives of the Tibetan saints or of the Castaneda-Don Juan legends: the master Vallejo must break down the disciple Eshleman to come into English; the disciple's ego resists; and ultimately the disciple learns from the struggle his own strengths, the strengths that will aid both the translation and the creation of his own poems.]

The other species are a rain forest of insects and animals, real and imagined; the poems *teem*. Yeats, in *A Vision*, writes of a man who, "seeking an image of the Absolute," fixes on the slug, for the highest and the lowest are "beyond human comprehension." Eshleman, however, in "The Death of Bill Evans," rejects interspecies apartheid to enter into slugness itself, transforming other into brother, finding an animal helpmate as guide to his meditation on the life of the jazz musician. And where many recent poets have resurrected Coyote and other indigenous trickster figures, Eshleman introduces into the poem, in a way that cannot be misconstrued as "pop," the contemporary American trickster, Donald Duck: the final image of the animal at the death of nature.

The geographical other is Eastern Europe (the suffering of imagination repressed) and mainly the Third Worlds of Peru, Southeast Asia, El Salvador, and South Africa (the sufferings of poverty and the imperial wars). It is the Morlock-Eloi vision of Wells' *The Time Machine*: Eshleman is one of the few poets to explore, beyond facile polemic, how "Indiana"—the comfort of the American middle class—is dependent on global misery, how the South African mines glitter from our wrists.

The invention of the historical other has become almost programmatic in twentieth-century American poetry: for Pound, ancient China; for H. D., classical Greece; for Olson, Mesopotamia; for Snyder, the Neolithic. Eshleman has pushed the historical back about as far as it can go: to the Upper Paleolithic, and the earliest surviving images made by humans. As a result of his literal and imaginative explorations of the painted and gouged caves, Eshleman has constructed a myth, perhaps the first compelling post-Darwinian myth: that the Paleolithic represents the "crisis" of the human "separating out" of the animal, the original birth and original fall of man. From that moment, human history spins out: from the repression of the animal within to the current extinction of the animals without; the inversion from matriarchy to patriarchy, and the denial of the feminine; the transformation of the fecund underworld into the Hell of suffering; and the rising of Hell, in the twentieth century, to the surface of the earth: Dachau, Hiroshima. The poet's journey is an archetypal scenario of descent and rebirth: he has traveled to the origin of humanness to reach the millennium, end and beginning.

It is Eshleman's confrontation with the personal other that has proved the most controversial. He is, surprisingly, probably the first poet ever to deal, in the poem, with the realities of infancy: not an allegorical "infant joy," but the drooling, babbling selves that are our private Lascaux. More noticeably to his detractors he has admitted what he calls the "lower body" into the poem: excrement, semen, menstrual blood. It has led *The New York Times Book Review* to wince, "He will not cooperate with taste, judgment, aesthetic standards . . ." (*cooperate!*) and an otherwise sympathetic critic to conclude that "Eshleman is not a happy man."

Such response reduces the poetry to an obsessive scatology, which it is not. On the contrary, one of the main drifts of the century has been the literal re-embodiment of the poem. Thus Williams, in "How to Write" (1936): poetry is "the middle brain, the nerves, the glands, the very muscles and bones of the body itself speaking." Or Olson's "Proprioception" (1962): "that one's life is informed from and by one's own literal body"; "Violence/ knives: anything to get the body in." If the facts of the lower body are prominent in certain Eshleman poems, they are always in context: an implied or apparent yoking with the upper body. It is the "amplitude of contradiction": face and ass, art and shit, menstrual blood and the blood of violence, each turning around and into the other in the poet's "yearning for oneness," the "challenge of wholeness."

Eshleman is the primary American practitioner of what Mickhail Bakhtin called "grotesque realism." It is an immersion in the body; not the body of the individual, the "bourgeois ego," but the body of all: the "brimming over abundance" of decay, fertility, birth, growth, death. As the collective body, it is unfinished, exaggerated; protuberances and apertures are prominent; animals, plants, objects, the world blend into its undifferentiated and essentially joyous swirl. The mask is its primary device: not as concealer of identity, but as image of each thing becoming something else.

Grotesque realism is "contrary to the classic images of the finished, completed man" (and to the finished, completed poem) "cleansed, as it were, of all the scoriae of birth and development." And it is contrary to what Bakhtin categorizes as "Romantic grotesque": the reaction against classicism which sought to restore the grotesque not in its original celebratory function, but as the malevolent underside of sunny classicism: the opening of the Pandora's box of aristocratic gloom, fear, repressed desire, and longing for death, where the ordinary "suddenly becomes meaningless, dubious, and hostile."

Eshleman's critics tend to read him in the terms of the Romantic grotesque, when his intent has been clearly the opposite. His grotesque is ecstatic and comic; through a systematic shedding of the oppressive weight of national identity and personal biography, he has taken the grotesque beyond Bakhtin's medieval carnival back to its source: the grotto, the cave. And there he has sought, and partially found, what Bakhtin calls "the complete freedom that is possible only in the completely fearless world."

It is precisely Eshleman's fearlessness that scares people off. ("He will not cooperate . . .") No other American poet has laid so much of his life literally on the line. It is illuminating, for example, to read Eshleman's 1970 poem on his father, "The Bridge at the Mayan Pass," alongside such celebrated, nearly contemporary poems as Robert Lowell's "Commander Lowell," Sylvia Plath's "Daddy," Allen Ginsberg's "Kaddish." In the case of Lowell and Plath, it is difficult today to imagine what all the fuss was about. Lowell's poem on his father depends on a safe titillation—the eccentric side of a well-known family—much like his "confessional" poems, which carefully reveal a few autobiographical details shocking to polite society (Mr. Lowell takes tranquilizers, Mr. Lowell was in the bughouse) without saying much at all. Plath has a cloying "more neurotic than thou" machismo; its scandal is a "nice girl" calling her Dad a vampire and a Nazi. Ginsberg's frank autobiography, still startling to read, serves a similar, elitist "band of loonies" function: this is what has made me crazy, this is my admission ticket to the "hipsterheaded angels." Eshleman, however, never wears the proud badge of neurosis. His violent, extremely disturbing rant is intended as a sign of health: the dismantling of the father (and the father in the son) as Indiana, that which denies life. It is an act of making love on the father's freshly dug grave.

Fearless too is Eshleman's language: dense, gluey, wildly veering from the oracular to the burlesque, strewn with neologisms and weird bits of American speech (*cruddy, weenie, chum, goo; tampax* as a verb). An Eshleman poem is unmistakable from the first glance. Image jams against image, not impressionistically, but in the service of a passionately argued line of reason, a line where an idea, before completion, turns into another idea, and then another, much like the walls of the Paleolithic caves. ("Image is crossbreeding/ or the refusal to respect/ the single individuated body.") The poems are nearly impossible to excerpt.

It is surprising that none of his critics seems to have noticed that Eshleman is, at times, extremely funny. Where else would one find, in the same poem, Apollo, Persephone, Ariadne, and "Silk Booties & Anklets Knit Soaker & Safety Pins/ Hug-me-tight a Floating Soap Dish with Soap Rubber Doggie"? With minor (usually stoned-cute) exceptions, the idea of the comic poem has become so alien to American poetry—who today thinks of Pound as he described himself: "a minor satirist"?—that the poet runs the serious risk of appearing foolish.

It is a foolishness measured by the last vestiges of the distinction between "poetic" and "unpoetic." Wordsworth, despite his championing of the life in common things, went to elaborate lengths in one passage of *The Prelude* to avoid writing the words "tic-tac-toe" (or "naughts and crosses"). To a certain extent that reticence still holds. To bring Floating Soap Dishes and Rubber Doggies—weird artifacts of the popular grotesque—into the poem's art aerie, to place Francis Bacon and Little Lulu in the same phrase, remains, in poetry at least, an act subversive to "taste, judgment, aesthetic standards." For Eshleman, Little Lulu is the lower half of Francis Bacon's body; to incorporate the two is the work of a comic wisdom.

It is a poetry and a life conceived as a "name encanyoned river" (Eshleman's turn on a Vallejo phrase and the title of his *Selected Poems*): a river that springs up in the arid wilderness of Indiana and flows toward a Utopic vision of personal and global wholeness; a river that is nearly all rapids and is flanked by canyon walls. Along the way one writes, paints, leaves one's mark on the walls: both an act of testimony for the community (this is where we are) and an imaginative leap to the other side.

Eshleman's totems for the journey have been the two insect spinners: the spider and the caterpillar. Both draw their art entirely from their own bodies. For one, the web: constructed with astonishing mobility, slung from branch to branch, a net almost all air, through which the world is visible beyond, in which the stuff of the world is randomly trapped. For the other, the cocoon: immobile, opaque, the prison where, in utter solitude, one effects transformation. What better allies could a poet have?

[1985]

Peace on Earth

January, 1982: It is ten years and a month since the Christmas bombing of North Vietnam—that genocidal frenzy of an army facing defeat. I am reading the day's paper: the former U.S. Ambassador to Laos protests that the secret spraying of defoliants over that country in the 1960's (revealed only yesterday) was no secret at all: "Rather, it was not admitted nor confirmed." It is the day's version of the same stories I have been reading every day of my reading life—a reading life sustained, in this enameled garden of meaningless language, by poetry; by the belief, perhaps a wild belief, that there is a general sanity in the work, a sanity that rises above the notorious small madnesses of the workers themselves.

And today I am reading a long poem called "Peace on Earth" by John Taggart, a poet of my generation—that well-publicized, self-publicized generation of '68: born during or after *the war*, who came of age in another *the war*, and who live there still. I am reading what, for the moment, is still an artifact of the moment, and I wonder how he, I, we, have arrived here; for this is our Peace on Earth:

> To delight friends with babies charred in napalm

* * *

Since the Napoleonic Wars there has been no narrative, no epic war poetry in the European languages that dealt with contemporary wars. There has been only antiwar poetry and, particularly in the American and Spanish Civil Wars, some battle hymns and calls to arms. Modern warfare has largely eliminated the warrior-hero, the only subject of epic, and replaced him with the tactician: an unheroic figure, usually removed from the battle itself, who brilliantly or stupidly maneuvers the slaughter of faceless legions.

137

As yet there is no poetry of tactics, but in English there have been two great clusters of antiwar poetry. The earliest grew out of World War I, the first war in which a large number of poets participated, and only the second war in history fought mainly by literates. [The first was the American Civil War, and the fact is commemorated in an unprecedented title: Melville's "On the Slain Collegians." Two poets of interest, Lanier and Timrod, fought for the South, while Whitman dressed the wounds of Northern soldiers in a Washington hospital.]

The poetry of World War I was, above all, written out of camaraderie. The men were sent into battle as a company, and returned, if at all, as a company. At the front, they were thrown into scenes of unimaginable horror, yet they never knew—for there was no explanation, and still is none—why the enemy was their enemy. The result, in fact and in the poetry, was a communal rage—at the carnage, the officers safely behind the lines, the comfort and platitudes of those at home—but also a great compassion, toward each other and even across the barbed wire. Wilfred Owen's most famous line was first written as: "I was a German conscript, and your friend." The key word is *conscript*: we are (were) both unwilling victims. In the second version of "Strange Meeting," Owen raised this perception to the immediate and the universal: "I am the enemy you killed, my friend."

In contrast, the work of those who stayed at home seems petty, oblivious. (Excepting the seventy-four-year-old Hardy, listening to the big guns across the Channel: "The world is as it used to be . . . Mad as hatters.") The "War Number" of Ezra Pound and Wyndham Lewis' *BLAST*, for example, is mainly devoted to attacks on Marinetti and the Futurists. Pound contributes some of his weakest satirical verse, and Eliot his impressionistic, apolitical "Preludes" and "Rhapsody on a Windy Night." Only Gaudier-Brzeska's message from the trenches gives any sense of what is occurring not so many miles away. The sculptor picks up a German mauser and breaks off the butt to carve—to have something to carve, to carve something. He writes: "*MY VIEWS ON SCULPTURE* REMAIN ABSOLUTELY *THE SAME*," and, in the context, we know that his conviction has not been easily won.

But Gaudier-Brzeska is also filled with idiocies: "THIS WAR

IS A GREAT REMEDY . . . IT TAKES AWAY FROM THE
MASSES NUMBERS AND NUMBERS OF UNIMPORTANT
UNITS . . ." The Vorticist position, if it can be called a position,
becomes clear some years later in Canto XVI: the war killed one
genius (Gaudier-Brzeska), inconvenienced some others, and
generally broke up the old gang. Pound's "And because of that
son of a bitch/ Franz Joseph of Austria . . . / They put Alding-
ton on Hill 70 . . ." is the war as literary event. It is not the war of
Isaac Rosenberg's "A man's brains splattered on/ A stretcher-
bearer's face." Though Pound is the greater poet—only five years
older than Rosenberg, he also had 50-odd more years in which to
write—any attempt at understanding his attitude to the war must
account for the fact that it was Pound who suggested to Rosenberg that he ought to enlist.

Other than those two monuments erected in the ruins—H. D.'s
Trilogy and Pound's *The Pisan Cantos*—World War II produced
little poetry in English still worth reading. Its major works were
narratives—novels and movies—which tended to explore the psy-
chological effects of war on a miscellaneous collection of individuals, the platoon. There was no, or hardly any, anti-war poetry,
for the rage and compassion of World War I were absent in a war
that almost everyone felt worth fighting. (Basil Bunting, for one,
was imprisoned as a conscientious objector in the First World
War, but hurried to join the Second.) Nor were there the rallying
cries of, say, the Spanish Civil War. Populist rallying, broad
satire, outrage were not exactly the stuff of poetry according to
the prevailing poetic mode of cleverly wrought ambiguities.
Nor—and it is shocking—did events affect those modes. Here, for
example, is Randall Jarrell (himself a combatant) turning a
concentration camp into rhyming couplets:

> Here men were drunk like water, burnt like wood.
> The fat of good
> And evil, the breast's star of hope
> Were rendered into soap.
>
> I paint the star I sawed from yellow pine—
> And plant the sign
> In soil that does not yet refuse
> Its usual Jews

[Jarrell, by the way, found it necessary to annotate these two stanzas for the 1955 edition of his *Selected Poems*: "Jews, under the Nazis, were made to wear a yellow star. The Star of David is set over Jewish graves as the Cross is set over Christian graves."]

And from the progressive flank there was mainly silence: Oppen and Bunting, in the middle of their long periods of not writing, were both soldiers. Williams begins his introduction to *The Wedge* (1944) with the statement, "The war is the first and only thing in the world today," and makes a plea for the relevancy of poetry. But the war enters the poems only occasionally, and always obscurely: something about violence being necessary to extract the meat from a nut, or:

> The bomb-sight adjusted destruction hangs
> by a hair over the cities. Bombs away!
> and the packed word descends—and
> rightly so.

or:

> No, not the downfall
> of the Western World
> but the wish for its
>   downfall
> in an idiot mind—
> Dance, Baby, dance!

The war runs in and out of Rexroth's *The Phoenix and the Tortoise* (1944), most memorably in the image of the terrified children discovering the body of a Japanese soldier washed up on the beach. MacDiarmid's *Lucky Poet* (1943) has a few bits of doggerel; Zukofsky's *Anew* (1946) barely mentions the war at all. Reznikoff's response, *Holocaust*, was to come thirty years later.

It was of course the Vietnam War that led to the greatest outpouring of antiwar poetry in English. Unlike World War I, this poetry was not written by combatants, for those who actually fought were unlike any soldiers of previous wars. [And could never be understood by old soldiers. Robert Graves on Vietnam: "Few of the unmaimed survivors will regret their part in this war."] They were boys—average age nineteen—without wives, children, higher education, careers. They were the first soldiers, ever, to be shipped out as individuals rather than as a company. They went, not, as in previous wars, for the cause or for the money, but out of fear of the punishment for not going. Once there, their fear—of the army, of death, of the strange land—was manipulated and transformed into racial hatred, a policy—and it was a policy—that finally permanently destroyed its own men. It was a hatred that blurred the lines between Vietnamese allies and enemies, national boundaries, soldiers and civilians, until the enemy became Asia itself, unconquerable, the symbol of every-thing that is "not us," that refuses to become us. Those who survived returned as solitary individuals to a country that ig-nored or hated them, where the only soldier who was not un-known was Lieutenant Calley.

The poetry of the Vietnam War was written at home, but curiously those who fought *against* the war were in a situation similar to that of those who had fought *in* World War I: they were a community united by disaster. Similar, that is, with one tremendous difference: it was a disaster the community had not experienced directly. Vietnam was never, and has never been, more than words in a newspaper and pictures on a television screen. The poets' Vietnam is a metaphor of a metaphor.

It was a poetry of contempt and communion. Away from the war, the poets directed their rage not at war itself (as in World War I) but rather at what was immediately at hand: those they suspected to be the instigators and supporters of the war—not the fat-cat industrialists of wars past, but, surprisingly, the ordinary middle-class suburban American. Read today, some of the most ardent of the "antiwar" poems seem merely the work of snobs, a dull continuation of the old Beat-Square friction. What is inter-esting, however, about these anti-"straight" antiwar poems is that they replicate exactly the most jingoistic prowar poems of other ages: lampooning the enemy for its looks, dress, food, taste; praising its own people for their superior wisdom, sexual ability, music, and so on.

But the other side of that contempt was the deep sense of community among those against the war, and the important position of poets and poetry within that community. Neither has existed since. It resulted in a poetry of celebration, love, ecstasy: the (now pathetic) declaration of a new age. Surely one of the most beautiful of these poems is Allen Ginsberg's "Genocide" (which has not dated, as his better-known "Wichita Vortex Sutra" has). In it, the poet dreams that he and (the then) Leroi Jones are naked in each other's arms:

> . . . He wanted
> to protect me in the War
> storm, but was unable
> for the great force that was
> upon us, of strangeness and
> alien white mind in America,
> rising from Iowa, Kansas,
> Nebraska, Wisconsin, Brooklyn.

Jones, at the time, was in his militant anti-white/Semitic/gay phase, and Ginsberg's poem is a vision of the peaceable kingdom, lion and lamb lying down together. It is the Vietnam revision of Owen's "Strange Meeting": we are both conscripts in this madness.

Two artifacts from the period are exemplary, both issues of important little magazines from a time when little magazines were important—were the voices of the culture: *Some/thing* #3 (1966) edited by David Antin and Jerome Rothenberg, and *Caterpillar* #3/4 (1968) edited by Clayton Eshleman. *Some/thing* #3, a special "Vietnam Assemblage" issue, features a cover by Andy Warhol: a perforated sheet of postage stamps, each stamp depicting a yellow button that reads "BOMB HANOI." *Caterpillar* #3/4 is a regular issue—none of its 270 pages are particularly war-related—but halfway through there are two photographs, captioned only as "Two 12-year-old Vietnamese girls burned by American napalm." They are unquestionably among the most horrible, indelible photographs I have seen.

The *Some/thing* cover was widely admired at the time. Its irony, like all irony, required and enjoyed a cognoscenti who understood that "BOMB HANOI," though a real button worn in sincerity by many, was not a sentiment shared by poets. But more important, its humor—now somewhat dim—is indicative of a development that had a greater effect on poetry than the news of atrocity: It seemed, then, that all the words had lost their meanings. The Vietnam War was the era of Pentagonese, of "friendly fire," of "in order to save the village it was necessary to destroy it." Half of the *Some/thing* issue is taken from the newspapers, and countless poems were composed out of that profusion of jargon-couched lies. In the absence of the war itself, the poets could only work from the words of the war. As Robert Duncan wrote in the magnificent "Of the War" section of *Passages*, the war had become "the bloody verse America writes over Asia."

There were two responses to that bloody verse. To attempt a Confucian rectification of names, fighting the language back toward meaning, or to revel in the free-floating signifiers through satire or collage. The latter course was naturally easier, especially as the political stance of the poet could be assumed without proof. But when a "BOMB HANOI" could be either funny or bloodthirsty, depending on its writer, it meant that the word had entirely become the invention of its speaker—a solipsism that erased the social contract of language.

Meanwhile, in Vietnam itself, things were real enough, and language—despite the clouds of official euphemism, another legacy of World War I—meant what it said. For years the most popular song on GI jukeboxes was not the baroque surrealism of Dylan or Lennon or acid rock; it was this bit of plain speech from The Animals: "We gotta get outa this place." It was a place few poets could take, even secondhand. When *Caterpillar* published the napalm-victim photographs (which had already been rejected by the leading left magazine of the time, *Ramparts*) it was generally thought, as I remember, that the magazine had gone too far.

Ten years after the Christmas bombing, the war continues, both there, in the ravaged land, and here, in the ravaged bodies and minds of the 2.8 million Americans who "served" in Vietnam. Possibly as many as 2.4 million of them were exposed to the dioxin-laced defoliant, Agent Orange. Many of them have suffered or will suffer—and the probability may be the greatest suffering of all—from various cancers, fatal liver dysfunctions, sterility, miscarriages among their wives, birth defects in their children. 100,000 of them have been imprisoned since the war; only 22% finished college. Their rates of suicide, drug-addiction, alcoholism, divorce, and mental breakdown are extremely high. The statistics clatter on: these are among America's most miserable, and their physical and mental devastation, mirror to the land they left behind, has been nationally forgotten, abandoned to the professional doers of good.

For the poets, too, Vietnam is a forgotten subject. [In fact most of the Vietnam poems were written from 1965 to 1969; they had stopped being written long before the war ended. Was there no longer anything to say? Had the general national antiwar sentiment weakened the necessity for the poetry? Or did the poets simply lose interest when they lost their vanguardist positon?] Unlike World War I, there has been, so far, no important work written after the event. Vietnam's only legacy to poetry may be that current obsession of the best minds of my generation: non-referentiality. Raised on the empty and mendacious language of the war, they now celebrate that emptiness. It is a despair masked by theory, and one that can only thrive in the tranquility of academic backwaters—as Dada flourished in neutral Zurich during World War I. The curiosity, though, is that these poets of non-referentiality consider their work to be political: the language of the new age, a blow against the word as capitalist commodity, "meaning" as "market value." But this is merely café Marxism—one need only imagine the fate of a non-referential poet almost anywhere outside of this country and Western Europe.

And yet, here is John Taggart's "Peace on Earth": perhaps the first poem of interest to come out of the Vietnam War in a decade, written by one of the brightest of the "younger" poets. And what is it?

Its compositional procedure, which is complex, must first be described: The poem is in three parts containing, in order, three, nine, and twenty-seven sections. Each section, printed one to a page, consists of thirteen lines in three stanzas of eight, one, and four lines each. The one-line stanza remains the same throughout each part, and each section within each part rings small changes on the preceding section. Thus the poem is read vertically, but also horizontally, as the reader inevitably compares, say, line eleven with the next section's line eleven. Quotations from *The Winter Soldier Investigation*—a book frequently cited during the last years of the antiwar movement—and, for no apparent reason, a Tarahumara healing song ("sana tafan tana tamaf tamafts bai") are embedded in the text.

Here is a typical section, from the second part:

> To delight to delight those who are friends to
> delight friends by turning by turning
> in a space *in nape, which is*
> *napalm, which the military*
> *likes as incinder*
> *jell after the fires burned down and*
> *there was an old man lying on a cot, burned*
> *to death with his hands stiff in rigor mortis.*
>
> Carry torches, carry each other.
>
> To delight friends by turning burning hands in napalm
> to run burning in a circle
> to be a light running
> and burning to death in a circle.

The first stanza becomes, on the following page:

> To delight to delight those who are friends to
> delight friends by turning by turning
> *in nape, which is napalm, which the*
> *military likes after the fires burned down and*
> *there was an old man burned*
> *to death with his hands stiff in*
> *rigor mortis reaching*
> *for the sky in prayer or supplication.*

which then turns into:

> To delight to delight those who are friends to
> delight friends by turning
> *in nape, napalm, which the military*
> *likes and there was an old man burned to*
> *death with hands stiff in reaching*
> *in prayer or supplication*
> *forgiving us what we had done and*
> *there was an old woman lying dead curled.*

and so on. (The italicized lines are from *The Winter Soldier Investigation*.) The tenth line rings the following changes through this part:

To delight friends by turning in napalm

To delight friends by turning burning hands in napalm

To delight friends by praying with hands in napalm

To delight friends praying with curled hands in napalm

To delight friends with hands born curled in napalm

To delight friends with children curled in napalm

To delight friends with baby children in napalm

To delight friends with babies scarlet in napalm

To delight friends with babies charred in napalm.

Toby Olson, in an eloquent description of what seems to be the author's intent, has written that "Peace on Earth" is:

> . . . a poem whose movement is able to cleanse the dead of the politics that caused their death, resurrect their clean bones, and celebrate their passing . . . Its title, starting in irony and coming through to the literal, can be seen as a measure of its movement. Like the best religious music, it transforms those who give themselves to it. In the experience of this poem, we can mourn and celebrate the dead with feelings that are purified of anger and resentment; we can give their Spirit Image a place of peace outside and above politics and irony. What John Taggart has done for us . . . is a holy thing.

To excerpt, as one must, destroys the cumulative effect of thirty-nine similar sections. Taggart notes that he wants the poem to be read aloud (what poet doesn't?) and its effect has been compared to that of the "trance" music of current composers like Phillip Glass and Steve Reich. The problem, however, is that spoken poetry, no matter how "musical" ("by turning by turning) is not music. What lifts us up in the "new music" or in the sung repetition of religious formulae only brings us down in poetry: we are too accustomed to varied and idiosyncratic selections from the vast storehouse of the language. When those selections remain the same—in a poem or in a life's work—we lose interest. And in a poem that is evidently not non-referential, relying on sound alone, the reiteration of content—even with slight variations in the words themselves—simply cannot be sustained for very long. Louis Zukofsky's "Julia's Wild" is lovely, but it is twenty lines long; "Peace on Earth" lasts about forty-five minutes.

Worse, the frequent repetition of a word within the same phrase or context—when it is not sung—only deadens the words. When, during the Vietnam War, John Giorno or Jackson Mac-Low presented repetitive collages of newspaper words, the intention was mimetic of the contemporary media assault. Ten years later this is not the case—the assault is the same, but the words are different. To hear, today, the word *napalm* twenty-one times in the course of nine thirteen-line pages only strips the word— the most highly charged word of the Vietnam War—of its resonance, while ironically making us realize that, yes, *napalm* is one of the most beautiful words in the language.

By attempting to bury the word *napalm* and build a Victorian monument over its grave, Taggart may be, as Olson claims, cleansing the dead of politics and purifying us of anger. But I wonder.

First, what are small variations on the line, "To delight friends with babies charred in napalm"? The infinitive implies "Let us . . ." and we must assume that either the line is literal and idiotic ("delight friends whose babies are charred" or "offer charred babies to delight friends") or it is ironic, like Warhol's "BOMB HANOI" (which, so long after the fact, loses its black humor and only recalls a forgotten elitism) or it is a collage and only semi-referential (somewhat pointless, so many years later) or it is pure sound (which would be scandalous).

Second, Taggart was not in the war, and has probably never seen Vietnam, a napalm victim, or even napalm itself. This would be irrelevant if Taggart had been able to recreate the word in his (and our) imagination—to live through it as, say, Defoe lived through a plague year from before his birth. But in "Peace on Earth" *napalm* remains a word from a book—specifically *The Winter Soldier Investigation*—as the poem, above all, has been made from books (e.g., the Tarahumara song).

Third, because he found the word in the library, Taggart—as
many contemporary poets would—reads it mythologically. Napalm becomes the sacred, purifying flame. Which it was not.
This mistake has been made before, notably in Denise Levertov's
"Advent 1966," one of the most famous poems of the war. In it,
the poet invokes Robert Southwell's Burning Babe, an image
that is "multiplied, multipled" in Vietnam. Although the poet
insists on the difference between Southwell's Christ and the na-
palmed infants, the poem, this far, doesn't work: Southwell's
perfect *created* image cannot help but be more powerful than a
secondhand image of reality. That is, Levertov (and the reader
who knows the Southwell poem) has experienced the Burning
Babe directly, in a way that neither poet nor most readers have
experienced burning babies. But what finally gives the poem its
great force is the poet's juxtaposition of herself and Southwell *as
poets*: this is what he was permitted to see, and this is what I see.
The best Vietnam War poems took the poet as witness; the
weakest poems presented the facts or language of the war, spoken
by no one.

David Jones could mythologize World War I only because *In
Parenthesis* is also a work of directly apprehended luminous
details. When Isaac Rosenberg writes, in "August 1914," "What
in our lives is burnt/ In the fire of this?" he has earned access to
the sacred fire because, in the context of his other work and of his
life, there is no question of "sincerity."

Taggart was able to write this celebratory hymn not because
the time for requiem has come—the living gathered to sing for
the dead. Only certain political details of the war have passed—
the war itself is not dead, especially among the Vietnamese and
among the veterans. Taggart's hymn exists because for us, who
stayed at home and fought against the war, *the war was a festival.*
An Arcady ruled by death, but an Arcady still. That moment of
community—a community of poets, the community of the generation—has never come back. "Peace on Earth" is a nostalgic
vision of peace—even its title comes from the 1960's: the Coltrane
concert in Japan—a vision that belongs to us Luddites who
fought the war machine and thought we had won. It may be the
last of the old Vietnam War poems—a flowering manured by

dead peasants and by our dead contemporaries who were too poor or too guileless to evade conscription.

The World War I poet Ivor Gurney wrote: "There are strange Hells within the minds War made." If a new Vietnam War poem is ever written in America, it will be a descent into that hell. It will have to be written by a veteran or one capable of living in a veteran's brain—a poetry of one who has killed and was almost killed. And if a new Vietnam War poem is written by those of us who stayed home, it will have to acknowledge the truth of our paradise: that we delighted in friends while babies charred in napalm.

[1982]

The Bomb

"Things are even more like they are now
than they've ever been."
　　　　　　　　　　　　　—Gerald Ford

On May 26, 1982, there was a reading at Town Hall in New York
City to benefit the nuclear freeze movement. Organized by Galway Kinnell, it was called, immodestly, "Poets Against the End
of the World," and it featured, inauspiciously, thirteen poets—
Amiri Baraka, Robert Bly, Jane Cooper, David Ignatow, June
Jordan, Kinnell himself, Etheridge Knight, Stanley Kunitz,
Denise Levertov, Phillip Levine, W. S. Merwin, Josephine Miles,
and Simon Ortiz—as well as the movie stars Jill Clayburgh and
Ossie Davis as emcees. It was probably the best-attended poetry
reading in New York since the Vietnam War. Town Hall was
sold out to an enthusiastic crowd of students who rose, at the
high point of the evening, to cheer Kunitz's poem on a beached
whale, which had been delivered in a Yeatsian high-pitched
drone. The drift of the reading was, as might be expected, "poetry
as life vs. the bomb as death." Practical considerations, and other
political issues, were largely skirted.

A year later the magazine *Poetry East* has published a special
number titled "Art and Guns: Political Poetry at Home and
Abroad," and it opens with a symposium on the Town Hall
reading, which the editors call "an important event in American
literary history." Most of the participating poets have contrib-
uted statements, and Kinnell is interviewed on the significance of
the evening.

Judging from the statements, the poets considered the reading
to be a valuable political gesture. Many of them compare it—in

meaning, not size—to the readings held against the Vietnam War. Baraka believes that the "social responsibility" and "positive stance" taken by the poets will lead to "dynamic, socially relevant poetry" in the years to come. Kinnell, in contrast, states that the nuclear issue is "so basic" that even a "non-political" poet can be "political" on the subject. Knight, covering both ends with a bit of candor, claims he participated because "1) my good friend, Galway Kinnell, asked me to, and 2) it was an opportunity for me to put my/ass/where my/words had been."

This needs some sorting out. First, the antinuke movement, as articulated by the poets at Town Hall and by the nearly one million demonstrators in the streets of New York two weeks later, was limited to an expression of disgust at the prospect of nuclear war. The rally and the reading were "against the end of the world"—an endorsement of the continuance rather than the extinction of the human and other species.

This is a philosophical position, not a political one. As such, it has attracted nearly everyone in the West from pacifists to mass-murderers like the CIA's William Colby—everyone, that is, except the masters of the nuclear arsenals. Contrary to Knight, it is attractive precisely because one does *not*, at this stage, have to put one's ass on the line. To be simply against the end of the world is not necessarily to challenge the state of the world.

The self-congratulatory tone of the reading and of the *Poetry East* statements—the delusion that the poets were actually *doing* something—is disheartening. At certain moments I tend to suspect, unpleasantly, that this is the first movement since the Vietnam War to generally capture the hearts of poets not because it is the paramount issue of our time, but rather, as Kinnell hints, because it allows the non-political to *seem* political, without affecting the poetry itself and without jeopardizing the American poet's recently acquired status as wage-earner.[1] The poet can continue to do exactly what he/she was doing before, but with an added veneer of irony or poignancy. If the Town Hall reading is any indication, then we're in for the same old poem about a daffodil, but now that daffodil will be seen in implicit (unspoken) contrast to the destruction of all daffodils. It's the same old poem about a beached whale, but now the beached whale is us.

Whether Baraka is correct—that the antinuke passion will lead to socially responsible poetry (not to mention action)—remains to be seen. The poets, on the evidence so far, are still at the stage of philosophical speculation: thinking about the unthinkable, choosing life against death. What is notably absent is political thought: how the end of the world is to be prevented; how the nuclear madness, while we are still alive, affects the lives of the poets and the life of poetry in this country.

The Town Hall reading benefited the groups that are endorsing a freeze in the production of nuclear weapons. It is an admirable, though rudimentary first step—in any other arena it would be dismissed as preservation of the status quo. If the freeze occurred today, it would still leave the world with some 10,170 American and 7400 Soviet nuclear warheads, not to mention those of England, China, France, India, and probably Israel and South Africa. Each of those warheads is from 1000 to 600,000 times the strength of the bombs that destroyed Hiroshima and Nagasaki; together, they could annihilate the populations of the earth and six or seven other earth-sized planets.

Obviously it is beyond the freeze that the poets and all of us have to think, for the disarmament of the world requires a kind of consensual transformation of global society that has never happened in our history—and, never having happened, seems as unimaginable as the extinction of the species. It is impossible to unlearn what we know—especially now that bomb technology is fairly simple—and impossible that the world will declare, along with a few poets and mystical adepts, that there is a Knowledge which should never be known. But it may be possible to end the Nuclear Age without blowing ourselves out of it. It would entail, however, the end of all nuclear activity, both military and domestic: not only the dismantling of the weapons, but of everything that requires or generates the uranium and plutonium that are necessary for bomb production.

More immediate—and with more concrete consequence to our lives—is the necessity to cure the psychosis that is driving us toward the war that will end all war and peace. For forty years the West, and particularly the United States, has been caught in a mass hysteria that all of us, believers and non-believers alike, suffer from daily: the madness of anticommunism. Not anticommunism as an intellectual position—the criticism of existing and potential political/economic systems—but anticommunism as a religious crusade, the equation of communism with the Enemy, with Satan.

We have our nuclear arsenal in the name of anticommunism; we kill, directly or indirectly, hundreds of people every day in shifting sections of the world in the name of anticommunism; we give billions to murderers abroad because any enemy of our Enemy is our friend. Our President believes that heaven itself is guarded by U.S. Marines (against whom?), that the Soviet Union is an "Evil Empire" where everyone is free to lie as much as they like because they don't believe in God. One fourth of all American children live in poverty because of anticommunism; our infant mortality rate is among the highest in the West. Because of anticommunism our government spends more on the food for the dogs of Army officers than on the school lunches for poor children. Because of anticommunism we play this global video game where, as in the arcades, one never wins but only postpones defeat.

Given the Manichean vision of this American (and Soviet, in its mirror image) madness, the obvious needs to be stated: To believe that the Marxist (or more exactly, Marxish) states have generally failed does not make one an anticommunist. And to be appalled by anticommunism does not make one a communist. Anticommunism is the delusion that there is an Other who must be destroyed if we are to live. Further, it is the delusion that there is no end to those Others, that any society may become, or already is, one of Them. Worse, it is a delusion we only partially or selectively believe. (Most notably: China, where yesterday's Peril is today's Potential Market.) At present we or our surrogates are murdering people in Guatemala, El Salvador, and Nicaragua to stop the "spread of Soviet domination." We supposedly fight these little wars because the big war is too terrifying. But—even if we accept the notion that every struggle against injustice originates in Moscow—do we really want to defeat or destroy the Soviet Union? If, suddenly, the Soviets had no nuclear weapons and we retained all of ours (or vice versa) it is doubtful that the political boundaries and structures of the world would change in the slightest. The result would be neither a tidal wave of commu-

nism or capitalism, but rather a flowering of the unnuked society, an economic prosperity irrigated by the flow of cash re-
channeled from useless to useful production.

Wars are fought for two reasons: 1) to repel foreign aggression,
and 2) to help business. (The second reason, with the notable
exception of the Opium War, is usually masked by ideology.) At
the moment, there may be hundreds of millions who detest the
U.S., but the U.S. has no active enemies. No one realistically
threatens our shores, plots the destruction of our government. (At
worst there is, abroad, bursts of small terrorist violences and
diplomatic and propagandistic attempts to undermine abstract
"influence.") For American business, the form of government of
a foreign nation barely matters. We are as happy trading with
Hungary as with South Africa, with Libya as with Switzerland.
(For their part, the so-called hostile nations are essentially hostile
only to American ownership of local enterprises.) With Coke on
sale, today, in Kabul, Tripoli, and Teheran, we cannot pretend to
be fighting to keep the world safe for American business. And
when we prop up the little demons in epaulets in Guatemala and
Chile and the Philippines, or attempt to "destabilize" popularly
elected or acclaimed governments, we are hardly fighting to
preserve democratic ideals. What we are doing is endlessly expanding our arsenal at the expense of our citizens and randomly
devastating sections of the globe for absolutely no reason at all.
We have become—there's no other word for it—insane, and it is
anticommunism that has driven us mad.

And where are the poets in all this? The same issue of *Poetry
East* includes a survey of literary magazine editors on the question of "poetry, politics and publishing." Their responses—
including, for god's sake, a favorable citation of Maxine Kumin's
"Poetry is too fragile an art for polemic"—fall into the usual
"good/bad politics does not necessarily mean good/bad poetry"
conundrum. The thinking moves in one direction: how politics
does or does not serve poetry. That poetry may serve politics is
not considered, nor the possibilities outside the poetry-politics
bind: namely, that the poet is also a citizen (capable of activities
other than writing poetry) and that the poet is also a writer
(capable of writing something other than poetry).

There are of course no answers, only individual solutions. But it is interesting to consider the exemplary and extreme cases of the poets who took the monastic vows of the Communist Party in the 1930's (and who found there the simultaneous freedom and repression that Thomas Merton found in his Trappist Order). Most of them—Hikmet, MacDiarmid, Neruda, Hughes, among so many others—chose to write political poetry: cries of rage or exhortations to arms. Some of it remains poetry worth reading; much of it does not. It was a gamble that immediate effect could also have enduring value; a gamble undertaken in the belief that poetry, above all, served the cause. (Today, of course, "enduring value" itself is a dubious proposition.)

There were other solutions: César Vallejo chose to continue writing the poetry he wrote, hardly accessible to the masses and more artifacts of a political sensibility than political statements themselves, but he served the Party by turning out a great deal of dogmatic prose. It is a prose that could have been written by anybody ("The social revolution is being seeded with the blood and battles of the proletarian class, and the front which embodies that class is none other than that of the Bolsheviks, vanguard of the working masses") but the point is that Vallejo felt it had to be written, that it should be written in prose rather than compromise the poetry, and that it could be written without compromising the poetry.

Another position taken by a major poet and Party member was that of George Oppen, who chose to stop writing altogether, in order to devote his time to organizing:

> I didn't believe in political poetry or poetry as being politically efficacious. I didn't even believe in the honesty of a man saying, "Well I'm a poet and I will make my contribution to the cause by writing poems about it." I don't believe that's any more honest than to make wooden nutmegs because you happen to be a woodworker.

The performance of the poets at Town Hall makes Oppen's argument persuasive: "Here's my wooden nutmeg against the end of the world." But the example of certain poets during the Vietnam War proves that it is quite possible to be simultaneously a political poet, a nonpolitical poet, a writer of political prose, and an activist citizen. There is no doubt that poetry honorably served the antiwar movement and, in its interaction of the arts and the political imperatives, the movement served poetry.[2]

The flowering occurred amidst, and because of, the flurry of self-criticism, self-doubt, and polemic about the role of the American artist in time of imperial war. That such criticism has not appeared among the antinuke poets is a sign of their complacency. We need to start thinking about what the Bomb has done to poetry—whether the question "After Auschwitz can anything be written?" has been supplanted by "Before Armageddon can anything be written?"

For one, the Bomb has destroyed the central myth all poets live by: "whether or not I am read today, future generations may read me." American poetry has largely been written for the unborn; nuclear war, more than the death of the living, means the obliteration of the future living—or, to speak for a moment from narrow self-interest, the abolition of a potential readership. It may well be that the denial of posterity has partially led to the current personality cults in poetry (and in everything else): the readings that are more stand-up comedy monologues than poetry, the magazines that feature photographs of the poets larger than the poems themselves, the absence of polemic and fear of toe-treading. [When the empire is in ruin—Rome, Tang China—the people become obsessed with immortality, life after death. When universal death seems imminent—the Plague—people become obsessed with the body and the self.]

Moreover, American poetry, especially that written by those born after 1945—the Irradiated Generation—seems to be written if not in an ivory tower then in a series of *gompas*: communities of like souls in remote mountain fastnesses. They are communities addicted to whimsey, nostalgia, preciosity. There is a longing for the days of Dada or Surrealism, a longing for the return of Coyote. Fleeting insights are netted and pinned to the page. On the aesthetic right, poetry is seen as a medium suitable only for anecdote and reminiscences of summer camp. On the aesthetic left, there is a talking in tongues, as though the Pentecostal fire had truly descended. It is, almost all of it, a poetry written from a Confucian wisdom—when the times are bad, head for the hills— that is no longer applicable. In the nuclear age, there are no hills, no world to be in reclusion *from*. Herakleitos is more to the point: "You cannot hide from that which will not go away."

We need to start thinking about the poets' dependence on the military state: the transformation, in the early 1970's from the poet as the traditional enemy of the state to the poet as the ward of the state, our private lives and our publications to a great extent dependent on government handouts—the few dollars that happened not to have been fed into the war machine. We need to reconsider the poets' role in the English Dept., working next door to the nuclear strategists. [For example, one of the better publishers of poetry these days, the University of California, is also the designer of *all* nuclear warheads.] We need to end our isolation, not from an abstract "the people," but from the world. [The last generation of poets to travel extensively in the Third World were those of the 1960 *The New American Poets* anthology.] The insanity of anticommunism can only be cured when America sees that the demon is human, as we have in China. We need poets as witnesses: to see the struggles for self-determination, to see the workings of the communist states, and to tell what they saw. We need to reassess our utilization of the small public we have: in the classrooms (if poets are to remain in the classrooms) and in the reading halls, and through our presses. [A small poetry publisher in England, Menard Press, is now devoting itself exclusively to antinuke material—a move I imagine most poets would find scandalous.] Above all, we need to re-examine the reigning dogma that what a poet does is write poetry. Otherwise, we remain up in the *gompa*, chanting into the wind until the firestorm blows the songs away.

[June 1983]

---

[1]When the poets get organized *as poets*, it's a sure sign that the literature is dead: The decline of the Troubadour tradition is marked by the founding of the Sobregaia Companhia dels Set Trobadors in Toulouse in 1323, of medieval Catalan poetry by the birth of the Consistori de la Gaia Ciència in Barcelona in 1393. Similarly, a magnificent half-century of American poetry ended when the poets allowed themselves to be organized and controlled by the two traditional enemies of poetry: the university and the state. A convenient date is 1970: the first publication of the *Directory of American Poets* (sponsored by the Nixon Administration and various multinational corporations and handily cross-indexed by race, it resulted in unlisted poets being refused work); the mushrooming of creative writing schools and college reading circuits; the introduction of contemporary poetry into literature courses and the purchasing by university libraries of

the "archives" of living writers; the first Black Studies and Women's Studies departments; the expansion of the National Endowment for the Arts and satellite organizations like the Coordinating Council of Literary Magazines and Poets in the Schools; the *Directory of Small Presses and Little Magazines, Coda* ("Poets read *Coda* the way bankers read *The Wall Street Journal!*" its ads proclaim) and other "service" publications—in all, the beginning of poetry as an acceptable, quasi-unionized, middle-class career in America. All this was coincident, not concidentally, with the end of anti-Vietnam War poetry (long before the war itself was over) and the end of Black Nationalist poetry.

To mourn the end of a golden age in American poetry is not to deny the presence of interesting and important poets—in fact quite a few of them—writing today in this country. A golden age is measured not by its peaks—there are always peaks—but by the mediocre. A third-rate Elizabethan poem is infinitely more enjoyable than a third-rate Augustan. Similarly, the standard fare of any avant-gardist magazine from the 1910's to the 1960's is far more engrossing than the typical reading matter of the last fifteen years.

[2]While the influence of the antiwar movement on ending the war remains debatable, it has recently been discovered that the movement inadvertently kept the world from blowing up. According to the memoirs of both Nixon and Haldeman, in the fall of 1969 Nixon instructed Kissinger to inform the North Vietnamese that if they did not accept his terms for a settlement, the U.S. would introduce nuclear weapons into the war. The deadline was November 1 and it was no bluff: the plans were drawn, and they included at least one target that was a mile and a half from the Chinese border. The North Vietnamese ignored the threat, and Nixon was persuaded not to carry out the plan for, he claims, only one reason: the October 15 Vietnam Moratorium and the November 15 Washington March Against Death. He correctly perceived that the country would not tolerate such a move and, as he tells it, the war then dragged on for years later, thanks to the antiwar movement. Seen from the other side, had there been no antiwar movement, global extinction might already have occurred.

The Modernists in the Basement
& the Stars Above

We can go by that door a dozen times
in a day and do that for years, maybe, without
thinking what's in there, paying it any heed
or needing to: why look in?
It's as much as though the room weren't part of the house
though we know, of course, it is; we think of it
in passing and dismiss the thought. Other times
prompted perhaps by some occurrence, we pause
to consider whether it might be better to sort
things over there. Maybe throw some out.

Aren't we the strong ones, though, aren't we here
as masters of the house! We are, indeed, until
one day we come by the door or where the door was once
and the door is gone. In the fetidness of the air,
we can barely breathe. Something nourishes,
as a plant might, in the dirt of the floor, grows
in the light from the window or in the dark at night.
Horror is what it is called. It is the whole
strength of the house, will be there when we move out,
hang deep in the cellar-hole when the house is gone.

—William Bronk
"The Strong Room of the House"

There are two stages of American horror. The first is the terror of
the forest, the "savages" who lurk just beyond the settlement
clearing in Hawthorne or Parkman or Chapman or the captivity
narratives. In the second stage, the forest is gone, but the architec-
ture of progress still contains, usually somewhere in the founda-

tions, a forest within. In Poe and Lovecraft, in countless American movies and in this poem by Bronk, there is horror in the basement: demons, a woman buried alive, a stairway to an ancient civilization; perhaps the house, like America itself, is built over an Indian burial ground.

To read American poetry—to spend a life reading American poetry—is to continually walk past that basement door, forgetting about it for months on end, and then suddenly to be startled to find it slightly ajar, to remember that there are demons in the house. One of them is hate: the hatred of mass man, manifest as a public loathing of ethnically, sexually, or socially delineated segments of the population. And the other, its twin, is megalomania: the delusions of power, wisdom, illumination. They are, as much as possible, not talked about. And yet to read, alongside the poetry, the essays, letters, and biographies of most of the twentieth-century American poets is to experience both exhilaration and dread. It is a walk in Rapaccini's garden of poisoned roses.

It is Ezra Pound—inescapably the center, the wobbling pivot of American poetry in this century—who, above all, embodies both the flower and the venom. Not the "suburban anti-Semite" he confessed to Allen Ginsberg, he was a lifelong, obsessive, paranoid hater of Jews. Had his cultural nexus been northern Europe rather than the Mediterranean, had he not towed so literally the Greco-Roman-cradle-of-civilization line, he could as easily have been a Nazi as an enthusiast for Mussolini. (During the war he signed some of his letters with swastikas and "Heil Hitler!"; in his radio broadcasts he recommended *Mein Kampf* and called Hitler "a Jeanne d'Arc, a saint.") His hatred of blacks extended to support for the White Citizens Council (for whom he wrote pamphlets), the Ku Klux Klan, and other such groups while he was in St. Elizabeths in the 1950's. There's no question that John Kasper was acting with Pound's blessings as he instigated race riots through the South, bombing newly integrated elementary schools.

None of this is news and yet, so long after the fact, Pound readers still fall into two mutually exclusive camps. Those who loathe him dismiss the poetry by referring to the politics and to the bigotry. Those who love him steadfastly read the literary works, keeping their eyes on the palaces in smoky light and the great ball of crystal, never glancing at what had fertilized such growth. In the thousands of elegant and erudite pages of *Paideuma* (the "Journal Devoted to Ezra Pound Scholarship"), for example, Pound's fear and hatred of Jews, or his relationship to types like John Kasper, is never mentioned.*

The official line has remained largely unchanged since the 1948 Bollingen Prize controversy. Pound was not an anti-Semite: he was using Jews as medieval symbols of usura, he was only attacking certain rich Jews—and didn't he promote Louis Zukofsky? Pound was not a Fascist: he (unfortunately) admired Mussolini, the drainer of swamps and enforcer of RR timetables. As for the broadcasts: he did not commit treason, but was merely airing economic views which he (right or wrong) thought would save America. Besides he was crazy—that is, too crazy to be tried for treason, too crazy to be held responsible for his social views, but not crazy enough to be locked up for a dozen years.

A few hours spent with the transcripts of the radio broadcasts (or the letters from the time, or the essays) will forever evaporate any lingering doubts about his anti-Semitism and his Fascism. They exist, were virulent, and were intrinsic to his life and work. Concern over Pound's treason requires both a nationalistic ardor, which is difficult to muster, and sufficient lack of confidence in the nation to believe that an individual far outside the power structure could cause serious damage. Nevertheless, Pound unquestionably favored the enemy in time of war: he wanted a Fascist Europe, if not a Fascist United States. Treason, however, implies effective actions (or the intent to perform such actions) in support of the enemy. To my mind, the broadcasts were not treasonous simply because they were useless, as the Italians well knew. One has to be familiar with the entire Pound pantheon,

---

*Worse, *Paideuma* appears to welcome those who are not unhappy with Pound's politics. One regular contributor will often stop a scholarly note dead in its tracks to defend the honor of Franco and Pétain, or declare the Guernica bombing a hoax. Another, a decade after the Vietnam War, is still making cracks about Jane Fonda. The editors, no doubt behind the "honorable gentlemen with diverse views" façade, seem strangely reluctant to red-pencil such extraneous matter.

from Confucius to the Malatestas, to begin to follow them. Even then the speeches are often incomprehensible. Whom could they have influenced? Perhaps a young Hugh Kenner, tuning in late at night on his (probably homemade) shortwave, but not many others. Pound was indeed crying "Fire!" in a crowded theater, but he was crying "Fire!" in Bulgarian.

In that, he probably was crazy: the belief that one is relaying information when nobody knows what you're talking about. And there is a case to be made—if one assumes that "democracy" is "health"—that Fascism itself is insane. But there is no doubt—and why do the Poundians try to deny it?—that he was not *legally* insane. Legal insanity means: 1) not in one's senses when one committed a crime; or 2) unable to understand the proceedings of one's own trial. The first is obviously inapplicable to Pound; and so is the second. [The latter a piece of law that is really quite touching: how much of one's other trials does one understand?] There is plenty of evidence, and no contrary evidence, that Pound throughout the St. Elizabeths years was completely aware of everything going on about him. That his responses could be unusual is beside the point. [Further, there's no question that Dr. Overholser, the head of the hospital, kept the law at bay by issuing misleading reports on Pound's condition. If he hadn't, Pound probably would have been executed. Rather than celebrating Overholser as a hero of quiet resistance to a vengeful government, the Poundians continue to deny his role.]

Pound's incarceration in the loony bin has long been used as proof of America's attitude to its best poets—an example that is extreme, but not entirely unfair. Yet curiously even the most orthodox disciples are coming around to a new reading of Pound's years in the hospital. It may well be that it was the happiest time of Pound's later life. He was without financial worries; he had full and uninterrupted time to write, a steady stream of people to talk to—after the isolation of wartime Rapallo—and a few young lovers. *Paideuma* editor Carroll Terrell even believes that if well-meaning friends hadn't sprung Pound he would have finished *The Cantos*. Instead, he was thrown back to his particularly messy life. And it was then, after he had left the hospital, that he broke down and fell into silence.

A small incident, something that came up the other day: As a follower of Chinese translation, I had known the work of one David Rafael Wang, a Chinese-American poet and a friend of Pound. Wang worked with William Carlos Williams on the translation of some forty Chinese poems in the 1950's. These ultimately appeared in *New Directions 19* (1966) with a note identifying him, improbably, as a direct descendent of Wang Wei. Paul Mariani, in his massive biography of Williams, mentions Wang twice (rather typically of the book, dropping "David" and spelling "Rafael" two ways): a passing reference, and later a paragraph describing Wang's visits to Williams and their collaboration. He cites a Williams letter to Wang on the beauty of Chinese poetry.

All very nice. Then, looking up something else, I happened to come across an article by David Rattray called "Weekend with Ezra Pound," published in *The Nation* in 1957, an extraordinary account of a visit to St. Elizabeths. In the course of the conversation Pound mentions Wang, and Rattray by chance knows him— as America's only Chinese white supremacist. It turns out that at the time Wang was traveling around the country setting up branches of the White Citizens Council on college campuses. Pound shows Rattray a letter from Wang, "filled with phrases such as 'the Cause which alone keeps body and soul together in this horrible city where all stinks of Jewry.'" Pound remarks: "Remarkably sensitive to the language for a young Chink."

Wang, I later discovered, was also the founder of the "North American Citizens for the Constitution," which demanded that Eisenhower and the Supreme Court be tried for treason for the desegregation rulings. He himself, of course, signifies nothing— at most he is a bizarre footnote to the "invention of China." What interests me, however, is that not only Pound (from whom we expect such things) but Williams and others were not merely tolerating but working with people like Wang in the 1950's—regardless of the daily reports of segregationist violence. That is, although Williams (unlike Pound) probably disagreed with Wang's extremism, his racism and political fanaticism were still considered as minor peccadilloes to be excused in the Artist.

Though less blatant (more genuinely "suburban") than
Pound, Williams' writing is also scattered with slurs which no
one thought to edit. There is a short story which begins, "He was
one of those fresh Jewish types you want to kill at sight, the
presuming poor whose looks change the minute cash is mentioned." And his essay "Against the Weather" asserts that Judaism is a "tribal-religious cult" that is "precisely the equivalent"
of Fascism—this written in 1939. Throughout the Mariani biography there are citations (without comment) of the Doctor on
Jews: "lewd Jew's eyes," "horrible overfed Jewish types," "some
fucking bastard of a yid," "some smart kike" (lawyer, that is, who
might try to sue him for libel), and so on. Yet Mariani, in the one
paragraph of his 900-page book that discusses Williams' racism
and anti-Semitism, brushes it off: WCW was "a product of his
times" who did not "always escape the popular racial myths of
his time."

And here is E. E. Cummings writing in 1950, after the war,
after the publication of the Dachau photographs:

> a kike is the most dangerous
> machine as yet invented
> by even yankee ingenu
> ity (out of a jew a few
> dead dollars and some twisted laws)
> it comes both prigged and canted

What is extraordinary is not Cummings' private loathings, but
that the Oxford University Press (on both sides of the Atlantic)
had no qualms about publishing the poem. Their only objection, in fact, was to the original last three words of the poem,
"pricked and cunted," which Cummings willingly changed.
How rarely did anyone along the publishing chain simply say no
to the dissemination of these fetid asides. How rarely were they
told to go publish somewhere else. The fact is that hate was part
and parcel of the American modern: an avant-gardist without
rage was considered emasculated; the object of the rage was irrelevant.

Pound, letter to Williams, 1936:

jews having been circumcised for centuries/ it must have had some
effect on the character. [. . .] history is written and character is
made by whether and HOW the male foreskin produces an effect of
glorious sunrise or of annoyance in slippin backward. Someone
diagnosed Shaw years ago by saying he had a tight foreskin/ the
whole of puritan idiocy is produced by badly built foreskins. Crimi-
nology/ penology shd/ be written around the cock. The dissecting
room shd/ lay off that chaotic bucket of sweet breads from the skull
and start research from the prong UPward. The lay of the nerves/
etc. This doesn't blot out endocrinology/ but it is the fount of aes-
thetics/ means microscopic attention/ dissection and micro/ photographic enlargements/ killers etc/ shd have their prongs photoed
postmortem.

Williams' reply:

. . . if cutting off the loose hide over a few thousand years has altered the Hebrew character—I doubt it. By all the laws of heredity
it should have affected the women and they are as bad as the men
today, or worse. It ain't the skin that makes the difference in the
man, its the stick in it that does it.

If there is a religion of the Pound Era, it is not Fascism, but
phallocentrism. Pound—despite his aversion to Hinduism,
which he considered more of a "mess" than Judaism—subscribed
to a quirky form of Kundalini, largely picked up from the writings of Rémy de Gourmont. According to Pound, the brain is
formed out of male genital matter, and creativity is dependent on
the flow of sperm from the testicles up the spinal cord to the
brain. (To facilitate the flow, Pound usually sat in a reclining
position, and built chairs for himself with backs pitched at 45-
degree angles.) Head and phallus are one—as in Gaudier-Brzeska's famous bust of Pound—and art-making is, quite literally,
ejaculation. Further, sperm-thought is pure light: the central
Pound metaphor is the resplendent monolith surrounded by
darkness.
[Williams adhered to a more primitive priapism: "Suppose all
women were delightful, the ugly, the short, the fat, the intellectual, the stupid, even the old—and making a virtue of their
qualities, each for each, made themselves available to men, some

man, any man—without greed. What a world it could be—for
women! . . . Take for instance the fat: If she were not too self-
conscious, did not regret that she were not lissome and quick
afoot but gave herself, full-belly to the sport! What a game it
would make! All would then be, in the best sense, beautiful—
entertaining to the mind as to the eye but especially to that part
of a man which we so mistakenly call the intellect . . . He would
be free, freed to the full completion of his desires."]

Robert Casillo has, quite brilliantly, connected Pound's phallocentrism and anti-Semitism. For Pound, circumcision deadened the phallus and was virtually the same as castration. He also
agreed with Hitler that Jews were the primary carriers of syphilis.
Jews then, with their numb or diseased genitals, were incapable
of imagination, and could only employ their evident intelligence
in life-denying manipulations of power, mainly the control of
money, the most lifeless thing of all. And of particular personal
terror to Pound was his Hebraic first name and the fact that he
looked Jewish, as Wyndham Lewis and others have testified—
that he might be mistaken for one of them, the "destroyers of
art." (Similarly, Williams suffered the embarrassment of having
a Jewish grandparent.)

That battle between an elite of "makers" and the "destroyers"
(or the indifferent) is the central myth of the American modern.
Pound expresses it in metaphors of light in the darkness, the
phallus of ideas driven into "the great passive vulva" of society.
Williams sees it as America vs. England (the latter oddly personi-
fied by a turncoat American, T. S. Eliot). For H. D.—see, for
example, her poem "Cities" in *Sea Garden*—the makers are a
beleaguered band of spiritual beauty-lovers, the last Hellenes.
For Eliot, they are Christian and Royalist, the standard-bearers of
the great tradition. Even on the left there was a fatal adherence to
group authority. Zukofsky invented a group, Objectivists, out of
nothing—a collection of largely disparate poets—and suffered
his whole life from self-perceived powerlessness as much as neglect. George Oppen remained an active member of the Communist Party through the Munich pact and the Gulag. [Others, right
and left, like Loy, Stein, Reznikoff, Stevens, Crane, Niedecker,

worked in a peculiar isolation—literary friendships without literary allegiances, a personal rather than a collective poetics, no political beliefs visible in the writings—much like many American poets today.]

It was, of course, a reaction to mass man, to the newly exploding population: half educated, sometimes actively hostile, and nearly always concerned with matters other than High Art. For Pound, the ideal audience was thirty readers. He even interrupts Canto 96 to declare: "One demands the right, now and again, to write for a few people with special interests and whose curiosity reaches into greater detail." (*Now and again*—as though normally the radiant gists were cast to the *lumpen.*) The rest of the world might as well be the character in Canto 28, who, espying the four folio volumes of Bayle's *Dictionnaire,* can only stammer: "Thass a funny lookin' buk . . . / Wu . . . wu . . . wot you goin' eh to do with ah . . . / . . . ah read-it?

The rest of the world was all niggers and kikes—a metaphor that became literal. Naturally one or two chosen ones from among these groups were allowed: Eliot's famous line that "any large number of free-thinking Jews" is "undesirable" implies that, well yes, if it must, a *few* would be all right . . . And among those few was Zukofsky, whose toadying to Pound extended to anti-Semitic cracks in his letters to the poet ("Do I luf my peepul? The only good Jew I know is my father: a coincidence") and the inclusion of Pound's "Der yiddisher Charleston band" in *An "Objectivists" Anthology.*

The Americans exalted the Artist while simultaneously making tragic generalizations about those they considered to be obstacles to Art. They, more than anyone, bought the "unacknowledged legislator" (secret holder of the power) myth. And they still do. From Pound's conviction that he could prevent World War II after a short chat with Roosevelt, to Olson's belief that he could *instinctively* decipher the Mayan glyphs, to the more recent equations of poets with alchemists, Kabbalists, and shamans, the rhetoric has continued while the poems themselves, like snail darters and furbish lousewarts, have retreated to the backwaters of the nation. When traditional visible/audible structures became hidden organizing principles and public utterance became private memoranda—when it became necessary to take the poet's not the poem's word on it—one was lucky to find even thirty readers.

Both the American (or more exactly, the Anglo-American) and the continental European avant-gardes were dependent on elite and misogynous brotherhoods: the "movements." Both expressed themselves primarily in military language. Yet despite Pound's passing interest in Dada—though mainly in Picabia as Artist—and Williams' occasional flirtations with France-in-New York, the objectives of the Americans and the Europeans were quite different. For the Europeans, it was a rebellion of the new art/anti-art against the old art; the enemy was culture, tradition, the academy, *art*. Under the banner of "life as art," they were particularly questioning the veneration of the art object and the idea of authorship (through readymades, collages of disposable and found materials, automatic writing, found poetry, dream imagery). Typical manifestoes would declare:

> Divert the canals to flood the museums! Oh, the joy of seeing the glorious old canvasses bobbing adrift on those waters, discolored and shredded!   (Marinetti)

> We should burn all libraries and allow to remain only that which everyone knows by heart. A beautiful age of the legend would then begin . . .   (Ball)

Where the European avant-garde was dismantling the received culture, their American counterparts were attempting to gather the live tradition from the air, to insert themselves into (European) literary history, to find historical validation—a struggle, more often than not, between art and the enemies of art, the yahoos and the messy ethnics, *people*. Under the banner "art as life," they believed in cultural restoration, purification of the language of the tribe (and purification of the tribe), a Confucian rectification of names, and an exaltation of object and maker. Where generally the Europeans shamelessly trashed traditional prosody, the Americans, performing similar operations, always invented historically based excuses—like the "ideogrammic method" or the "variable foot." The American avant-garde was attempting to become the next chapter of the Book of Western Culture—the book the European literary avant-garde was tossing in the river. Pound became a Fascist to restore the old order; Marinetti became a Fascist to destroy it.

[Curiously, the model for the European modern is nineteenth-century America: Thoreau and Hawthorne and Melville casting off the dead skin of Europe to declare that history begins again, *here*; Dickinson, dismantling and transforming the English poetic; Whitman, the subversive, the new mind casting the new line—the poet whom the Europeans and Latin Americans embraced while the Americans nervously looked the other way. This flowering died, of course, when James shifted the literary capital of the U.S. to London, and Pound began (and wrote much of) his tale of the tribe in the pseudo-archaic speech of pre-Raphaelite knights.]

In the end it may well be that Pound was a modernist in spite of himself. And because of his phallocentric "authority," because of his Fascism, his intrinsic anti-modernism, *The Cantos* continue to be read differently from any other twentieth-century text. The Poundians, as Pound intended, read the poem as an epic, and perform fantastic contortions to link it to the traditional epic. The success of *The Cantos* is measured according to classical unities; otherwise invisible structures and themes are stretched and stitched together. Some, like Pound, consider the poem to be a tragedy—for others a magnificent failure—because "it does not cohere."

Such expectations are not raised for the other American long poems of the century, despite their many similarities to *The Cantos*. No unifying devices are asserted for *Paterson* and *The Maximus Poems* other than their locations in a specific place (or for H. D.'s *Trilogy* other than its location in time of war); *"A"* is read simply as an autobiography in a planned and completed twenty-four sections written over the course of a life. And yet *The Cantos* remain an epic, a "long poem including history," and not what it is: an autobiographical poem of a man reading history, as coherent and incoherent, as random in its specifics, as any life. The strange fact is that perhaps the greatest modernist poem was written by an anti-modernist; it is not what it was intended to be at all.

There is indeed a fundamental contradiction between modernism and Judaism—the Judaism, that is, of the Mosaic laws, not the various heterodoxies. (It is a contradiction, I should quickly add, that has nothing to do with the anti-Semitism of the modernists; it was never articulated in their various rants, and does not "explain away" their behavior.) In the Judaism of the Mosaic laws the human yearning for wholeness manifests itself not in the universal admission of everything in the world (as in Hinduism) but in a loathing for that which is incomplete, mixed, other. A few examples among the hundreds:

Mixed: One cannot plant two kinds of crops in the same field, plow with an ox and an ass yoked together, breed cattle with a different kind, wear clothing made from two kinds of fabric, marry an outsider, eat meat and milk together.

Incomplete: A man missing any limbs or organs cannot be buried in sanctified ground. An animal with a "blemish" (maimed, disfigured) cannot be sacrificed. [In other societies the disfigured animal is particularly sacred.] A man with a blemish cannot be a priest. Any loss is a blemish, therefore semen, menstrual blood, and death (loss of breath) are unclean—a priest cannot go near a corpse.

Other: A norm is postulated, and any variance from the norm is taboo. Men are the norm: women must be segregated. Living creatures other than plants must move—animals must walk on four legs, birds must fly, sea creatures must swim with fins. Any animals that do not are unclean, such as most insects (six or more legs), lobsters (no fins), clams (seemingly immobile), snakes (no legs), etc. Further, the norm for animals is the ruminant with a cloven hoof (sheep and cattle): the others therefore are unclean.

These three qualities practically define modernism: its primary procedure, collage (mixed); its insistence on process over product (incomplete); its unending clarion calls to admit into poetry everything which had previously been excluded (other). In that, modernism was similar to early Christianity, whose disciples exhorted the people literally to "eat everything," and whose object of veneration was the ultimate hybrid: a man-god, child of the most blasphemous mixed union imaginable.

Furthermore, Judaism—as Christianity and Islam would later do—codifies intolerance. The story of the Exodus, to take the most obvious example, reads today like a Stalinist manual on the suppression of dissent.* As Mircea Eliade has remarked, the behavior of Yahweh was to become the "model and justification" for "the intolerance and fanaticism that are characteristic of the prophets and missionaries of [all] three monotheisms."

Pound's modernism, pantheism, and Hellenism are contrary to Judaeo-Christian-Islamic tradition. Yet, as a product of the monotheisms, he asserts his contempt in their very terms. Both Pound and the tradition are xenophobic; both believe in an enlightened elite. And, like the Christians and Muslims (if not the Jews), Pound believed that the others, no matter how damned, were capable of conversion. Whatever we think of the cause, he spent his life trying to persuade the world onto the True Path.

Octavio Paz has written that poetry is the secret religion of the twentieth century, and politics its public religion. For American poets, the public religion is in ruin—we must be the only country today where few writers are ideologues, or even interested. As for the private religion, it continues to be composed of initiates and no public, strict hierarchies of the faithful, petrified canons (orthodox and heterodox versions), secret codes, symbols, and texts. It is a religion that is two thirds Masonic Temple and one third Catholic Church, whose rival factions squabble behind the ponderous and forbidding walls of the sacred compound.

The European avant-garde's credo of art as subversion, art as the enemy of the state, which appeared only once in America in

---

*Throughout the story the Hebrews are complaining: they are sick of the hardships of the desert and want to go back to Egypt, where they at least ate well, even as slaves. When Moses comes down from the mountain and discovers the people worshiping the Golden Calf (a god they have collectively fashioned out of their own jewelry, rather than an authority imposed from above; and a god for whom the proper obeisance is celebration not sacrifice) his response is to strengthen the priesthood and initiate a purge; three thousand are killed. It takes them forty years to cross two hundred miles of desert, not because the Hebrews have such a lousy sense of direction, but rather because Yahweh and Moses deliberately keep them going in circles until all those who remember Egypt are dead and a new indoctrinated generation has taken over. Only then can they enter the promised land.

this century, during the Vietnam War—the revolutionary art of the 1930's basically sought to replace one state with another—has become almost laughable. Today *every* poet (and magazine and book publisher) in the U.S. is a ward of the state and the university, and the avant-garde's wrath at the institutions is limited to grumbles over the comparatively small slice of the pie they are being served. Even more disastrous than this economic dependency is the fact that poets have stopped talking publicly about poetry, that they are allowing the professors to speak for them, or worse, speaking themselves, when they do speak, in the language of "comparative literature." Today, the more radical the poetry, the more academic, jargon-struck, and convoluted the critical validation—much of it written by poets. American poetry has become a village with more anthropologists than Eskimos—a village where the Eskimos are making tourist art for their own consumption and can no longer tell a story without deconstructing their "belief system."

It may well be that the group of very fine poets born between 1935 and 1945 (Ronald Johnson, Clayton Eshleman, Clark Coolidge, Karin Lessing, Robert Kelly, Susan Howe, Gustaf Sobin, Rachel DuPlessis, Michael Palmer, among others) represents the last generation of modernism in America. It is not difficult to imagine that history, if it exists, will telescope the chronology and see their considerable accomplishments as of a piece with that of Pound, Williams, and H. D.; Reznikoff, Oppen, Zukofsky, Niedecker, and Rexroth; Olson, Bronk, and Duncan; and so many others.

And yet I can't help but feel that those of us born after 1945 were born—for all the obvious reasons—into another world, and that this generation has yet to find its poetry. Those in the universities have reduced poetry to anecdote and craftsmanship: a sometimes witty form of macramé which, at its best, follows the precepts of Imagism. Those who consider themselves "avant-garde" are restaging the battles of Russian Futurism and Dadaism under the banners of the latest linguistic hypotheses. The best literary magazines give much of their space to "archival material," and we hotly debate what Ez and Bill said or didn't say in 1922. And yet the historical distance between us and the pioneer modernists is the distance between "The Charge of the

Light Brigade" and "Hugh Selwyn Mauberly," between *Eugene Onegin* and *zaum*, between Hugo's major poetry and Tristan Tzara.

It is time for the modern masters to become ancestors, to become as ancient *and* contemporary as Li Shang-yin or Christopher Smart, Dickinson or Hölderlin, Ausias March or Ono no Komachi. In the current climate of hagiolatry and nostalgia, the demons of elitism and contempt that gave modernism its strength have been generally ignored. But they have not gone away. They are, I think, an obstacle between my generation and its poetry—a poetry that will not be "postmodern" (defined by modernism) but something that will come into being only when the great century of modernism is declared over.

For if an American postmodern is to occur, it will have to bring down the monasteries and cathedrals of modernism, and, like Hinduism, build shrines on every corner, honor a pantheon of thousands of gods with shifting attributes, and celebrate a calendar full of festivals and as many rites as there are practitioners.

It will have to pull down the mausoleums and monuments, exhume the remains, and place the skulls of Pound, Williams, Eliot, and all the rest on spikes at the gates of the city. That the citizens may look daily at these, the venerable ancestors, the monstrous poets, the magnificent poem-makers, architects of paradises, builders of infernos, collective source of a great power, the "strength of the house." The strength that is in the poetry not the poet, the power that still radiates from the poems unnoticed while the priests examine the entrails of dead poets for signs.

For the next flowering will come from the ashes of the Poet: a pyre kindled by manuscripts, letters, interviews, deluxe editions, archives, "collectible" relics. A pyre heaped with personality cults, irony, self-reference, "self-kleptomania" (Tzara), I the confessor, I the reminiscer, I the windbag, I the reader.

The disappearance of the poet, leading not to the "poem itself" (ahistorical, discrete, sanctified—like the Black Stone of Mecca) but a poetry written somewhere: a product of place and time, and yet a piece of local conversation that is spoken and heard in the universe of silence, a strange music coming over the water. Some of it, idiosyncratic voices attached to no particular bodies. Some, transparent voices elaborating idiosyncratic thought. Ideas *and* things: meditation and a new description of the world: *interesting* poetry.

Not to sever, at last, the link of signified and signifier, but the contrary: to move toward, never reaching, the mythic unity of the two—as in certain tribes, where to know the name of something is to possess it. A language recharged: not by souping up the synonyms, but rather through a hyper-referentiality, a recovering of the power of concentrated, musical speech. Mantra: magic. Centripetal melodies and centrifugal discourse: the world imploding into song *and* the poem spinning out into the world. A language not of dreams—Surrealism without its political context has become whimsey—but of bedtime stories: unforgettable speech propelling into private reveries. The wisdom of the reveries impelling action. A poetry of spokesmen and witnesses, I and you, birds and stars, us in the cities: subversive, informative, erotic, pantheistic, cosmic.

A poetry that recovers its original function as legal contract, prescription drug, birth-death-marriage certificate, public relations, prayer, weather and crop forecast, historical archive, good-luck charm, how-to-book, atlas, star chart, genealogical record, the evening news, the world almanac.

No longer the provider of entertaining puzzles for specialists, the poets returning to their traditional roles as icon-makers and iconoclasts, philosophers, historians, intellectual consciences, spokesmen for those who are not speaking (including nonhuman species), political commentators, natural scientists, makers of prayers and aphrodisiacs, officiants at the great transitions of life within a (decentralized) community each must create.

A poetry of essential service. A poetry that ratifies the social contract of language. A poetry that describes its world, its history, its cosmos. A poetry of celebration *and* condemnation of the stuff and the way of the world. Song, narrative, speech: people talking to the gods and to each other.

For some say that besides our sun, there is another sun. (They have named it *Nemesis*, and some even call it the *death star*.) Every twenty-eight million years this other sun enters the Oort cloud, that frozen halo of comets on the edge of the solar system. And more: within the Oort cloud, they say there is another cloud, ten times as dense, and this other cloud is the true source of comets.

This other sun, in its orbit, enters the cloud within the Oort cloud and pulls a billion comets loose; they scatter. For a million years, if one could watch from earth, the sky would be bright with a slow-moving fireworks of comets.

But some of them would strike the earth, and the dust thrown in the air by the impact would block out the sun for centuries. Little could survive such darkness, and little does. In the geological record, the book of earth, there are, every twenty-eight million years, craters, a layer of dust, and the remains of mass extinction.

And others say that there is no cycle, no twin of the sun, that the evidence has been misread.

[1984]